HIGH SPIRITS

High Spirits

A Round of Drinking Stories

Edited by

KAREN STEVENS

and

JONATHAN TAYLOR

Valley Press

First published in 2018 by Valley Press
Woodend, The Crescent, Scarborough, YO11 2PW
www.valleypressuk.com

First edition, second printing (November 2018)

ISBN 978-1-912436-12-5
Cat. no. VP0132

Pages 134-144: Tasting notes for Moet & Chandon Grand
Vintage 1988, quoted from site below (last accessed 1.10.2017):
https://www.champagnedirect.co.uk/deactivate_cat_prod.cfm

Cover and text design by Jamie McGarry.

Printed and bound in the EU by Pulsio, Paris.

Supported using public funding by
**ARTS COUNCIL
ENGLAND**

LOTTERY FUNDED

Contents

ACKNOWLEDGEMENTS

Thanks to the National Association of Writers in Education (NAWE); University of Leicester; University of Chichester; Jamie McGarry; David Swann; Maria Taylor; the 'Owls'.

DEDICATIONS

Karen: *for Alistair Smith – who loves a glass or two … or three …*

Jonathan: *for Helen Lingwood – long-time drinking buddy who doesn't drink.*

'To alcohol – the cause of, and solution to, all of life's problems.'

Homer Simpson

Introduction

by Karen Stevens and Jonathan Taylor

Now take the wine! Now it is time, companions!
Drain your golden goblets to the dregs!
Dark is life, and so is death!

– Hans Bethge and Gustav Mahler, *Das Trinklied vom Jammer der Erde*[1]

1. Beginnings: Discovery of the Drug

Literature's association with drinking, drunkenness and pubs is very old indeed. For Steven Earnshaw, in fact, 'English literature begins in a pub' – the pub, that is, at the start of Geoffrey Chaucer's *The Canterbury Tales* (1372-1400). 'The inn is a good place for English literature to set out from,' claims Earnshaw, 'because drinking places and literature have both been significant and pervasive in the development of the English nation and English consciousness.'[2] What Earnshaw implies is that the inn comes *first*: as a point of origin for Chaucer's pilgrims, the drinking place – and hence drinking in general – precede English literature in national consciousness. Drinking gives birth to literature, as it were.

Such an idea is not unique to English consciousness.

---

1 Quoted in Deryck Cooke, *Gustav Mahler: An Introduction to His Music* (London: Faber and Faber, 1980), p.109.

2 Steven Earnshaw, *The Pub in Literature: England's Altered State* (Manchester: Manchester University Press, 2000), p.2.

In Ireland, for example, the short-story writer Brendan Behan was famously described as 'the drinker with writing problems,'[3] implying that writing is secondary to, a problematic offshoot of, alcoholic consumption. On a more Nietzschean-philosophical level, the Russian critic Vyacheslav Ivanov argues in his essay *The Hellenic Religion of the Suffering God* (1904) that literature originated with Dionysus – the god of wine – and early Dionysian mysteries.[4] Ivanov and Behan might both have agreed with Monty Python's 'Philosophers' Song' (1970), in which René Descartes is heard to declare: 'I drink, therefore I am.'[5] Drinking, it seems, comes first – in philosophy, literature and consciousness.

It not only comes first: it also continues to haunt many, if not most, literary traditions throughout history. Drinking, drinking places and literature co-exist and overlap in the historical consciousness of many cultures. For example, Earnshaw mentions a 'long tradition of "bacchic" verse' in European literature, as well as the 'Arabic wine poem (*khamriyya*)';[6] and overlaps between drinking and literary culture are also obvious in Chinese, Egyptian, Japanese and many other parallel traditions – both in written and in oral forms.

3 Quoted in Peter Haining, 'Introduction,' in *Great Irish Drinking Stories: The Craic's the Thing*, ed. Peter Haining (London: Souvenir, 2002), pp.11-15, 14.
4 As Slava Yastremski writes, 'Ivanov ... summed up his Dionysian ideas in his treatise *The Hellenic Religion of the Suffering God* (1904), which traced the roots of literary art in general and the art of tragedy in particular to ancient Dionysian mysteries' (Slava I. Yastremski, 'Notes,' in Olga A. Sedakova, *Freedom to Believe: Philosophical and Cultural Essays*, trans. Slava I. Yastremski and Michael M. Naydan (Lewisburg: Bucknell University Press, 2010), p.134).
5 Monty Python, 'The Philosophers' Song: Lyrics,' http://www.metrolyrics.com/the-philosophers-song-lyrics-monty-python.html (last accessed 4.11.16).
6 Earnshaw, *The Pub in Literature*, pp.3-4.

The prevalence of '"bacchic" verse,' 'wine poems' and 'drinking songs' in many cultures has been much remarked on. There is, as Earnshaw points out, 'a … continuous generic line of … "drinking songs" or "Anacreontics" (verse in praise of love or wine)'[7] – and this is both a poetic *and* a musical tradition. From pre-Christian poetry to modern poetry, from Euripides to Shakespeare to Emily Dickinson to Robert Graves, from the ancient Norse tradition of Wassailing to folk songs to classical art songs, from Henry Purcell to Franz Schubert to Giuseppe Verdi to Gustav Mahler to Carl Orff, there are multiple, well-known traditions of both 'drinking songs' and 'drinking poems,' right up to the present day.[8]

What is slightly less well-known, but (we would argue) equally significant, is a tradition of drinking *stories*. After all, *The Canterbury Tales* is not just a work of poetry: it is also a collection of stories, which starts in a pub. Many drinking poems and songs throughout history also function as mini-narratives – as poetic short stories; and the literary 'short story' form as it has developed over the last two hundred or so years is bound up, in all sorts of literal and symbolic ways, with drinking, alcohol and alcoholism. Many well-known short-story writers have had drinking problems – or, to reformulate the description of Behan, many well-known drinkers have had short-story problems.

No doubt this is the case for many modern writers working in *all* genres and forms. In the West during the last two hundred years, drinking and drunkenness have not only been associated with texts, but also with authors. With the rise in the prestige of the author from the Romantic era onwards, drinking, drunkenness and other forms of

7 Ibid, p.3.
8 See, most recently, *One for the Road: An Anthology of Pubs and Poetry*, ed. Stuart Maconie and Helen Mort (Sheffield: Smith / Doorstop, 2017).

intoxication (such as opium addiction and drug abuse) have been commonly identified with the authors who seem to stand behind, or outside their own texts. Alcohol has, as it were, leaked out of texts and been imbibed by their authors.

Indeed, intoxication and alcoholism have become a kind of badge, a medal of honour, in a word a *sign* of the author, such that an author might be *expected* to have a drink problem, or something of that sort. Alcoholic consumption functions as a sign of the author's prestige, of his or her special insight, imagination, privileged kind of anguish, peculiar inner demons. There are various inter-linked layers to this sign, various interwoven implications: the author is an alcoholic because he or she experiences the pain of the world too keenly; or the author is an alcoholic because alcohol helps him or her to experience the world more keenly, see it in a different light. Alcohol is at one and the same time a mode of escape, a facilitator or inten-sifier of the imagination, and a sign of the author's indi-viduality. In other words: excessive alcohol consumption is somehow an expression of the author's privileged and individualistic position in relation to the world. Such an attitude is understandable in a world in which the author's individuality is always under threat: inebriation provides a handy antidote to the ever-increasing 'professionalisation' and institutionalisation of the author (by, for example, mass-market publishers, the media, universities) in so-called 'late' capitalism.

2. Middles: Addiction and Dependence

In late capitalism, many writers have happily or unhappily lived up to the expectation of perpetual inebriation. As Olivia Laing writes, in her wonderful book on the subject of authors and drinking, *The Trip to Echo Spring* (2013), there are numerous 'writers whose lives were made desolate by alcohol.' These include:

> John Cheever, ... Raymond Carver ... Ernest Hemingway, William Faulkner, Tennessee Williams, Jean Rhys, Patricia Highsmith, Truman Capote, Dylan Thomas, Marguerite Duras, Hart Crane, John Berryman, Jack London, Elizabeth Bishop, Raymond Chandler – the list staggers on.[9]

Clearly, Laing's list includes female as well as male writers, although the latter predominate, and there remains in circulation a powerful macho stereotype of the heavy-drinking male author, which might be traced back via the Beats to the early twentieth century, and beyond. If drinking is sometimes a sign of authorial individuality, it can also be a sign of a specifically *masculine* individuality: the 'heroic drinker' is often stereotyped as a male figure, whose drinking is an expression of his macho power, of his authority over others within what is traditionally a masculine space (the inn, pub or bar). Certainly, there have been a large number of male writers who have lived up to this stereotype: as well as those named by Laing, there is, for instance, the American short-story writer and heavy drinker Charles Bukowski, who, recalling his first introduction to

---

9 Olivia Laing, *The Trip to Echo Spring: On Writers and Drinking* (Edinburgh: Canongate, 2014), p.7.

wine, declares he felt that it was 'better than masturbating
… With this, … a man was perfect, nothing could touch
him … I … found something that [was] … going to help
me, for a long long time.'[10] Alcohol here is a sign of man-
hood and masculine inspiration: it is something which, in
terms both of masculinity and creativity, is 'going to help'
Bukowski the author. Such attitudes toward drink persist
through many of Bukowski's stories; in 'Beers and Poets
and Talk' (1972), for example, he reminisces 'about …
some of the women I used to know, some of the women
I had buried, outdrunk, outfucked … the alcoholic madwomen who had brought love to me especially and in their
own way.'[11] For Bukowski, it would seem that drinking
and fucking are competitive sports, in which the narrator (who is identified as a version of Bukowski himself)
demonstrates his masculine authority over women – even
'alcoholic madwomen.'

Bukowski is not the only short-story writer to see drinking, in particular, as a competitive and masculine sport.
Indeed, there are various short stories by other writers – including one or two in the following anthology – which,
either consciously or unconsciously, stage masculine drinking competitions. These include, for example, Mario Vargas Llosa's short story 'On Sunday' (1957), where the pro-
tagonist attempts to prove his masculinity by out-drinking
a love rival.[12] Not dissimilarly, Raymond Carver's story
'Why Don't You Dance?' (1981) stages what is, in effect,
a drinking competition between a middle-aged man and

10 Charles Bukowski, *Ham on Rye* (Edinburgh: Canongate, 2015),
pp.111-2.
11 Charles Bukowski, 'Beer and Poets and Talk,' in *Tales of Ordinary
Madness*, ed. Gail Chiarrello (London: Virgin, 2009), pp.135-8, 137.
12 Mario Vargas Llosa, 'On Sunday,' in *The Cubs and Other Stories*, trans.
Gregory Kolovakos and Ronald Christ (London: Faber and Faber, 1991),
pp.87-109.

a boy; the middle-aged man out-drinks the boy, and ends up dancing with the latter's girlfriend.[13] This situation is reversed at the end of 'An Afternoon Outing' (2012) by Panos Karnezis: in this story, a final beer symbolises a son's assertion of his dawning masculine power over and above an emasculated older man, who is presumably his father.[14]

If the association of literary culture with drinking competitions dates all the way back to symposia in Ancient Greece,[15] there are various structural characteristics of drinking competitions which lend themselves, in particular, to the modern short story form: the brutal competition between two men, sometimes over a woman (as is the case in Llosa's and Carver's stories); the conflict and sense of increasing tension, as those involved become steadily more drunk; the concentrated time-span, which, of course, is often fundamental to the short story form; and the inherent sense of narrative structure – of beginning (challenge), middle (competition) and end (defeat of one of the participants). In a wider sense, this is no doubt why there are so many stories about drinking in general: the consumption of alcohol of an evening necessarily implies a beginning (going to the pub, starting to drink), middle (drunkenness) and end (being sick, passing out, death, and so on). Drinking, the process of getting drunk, *is* a short story. Conversely, the short story *is* a kind of drinking: we get drunk on reading a story, as it were. A number of writers

13 Raymond Carver, 'Why Don't You Dance?,' in *What We Talk About When We Talk About Love* (London: Vintage, 2009), pp.3–9.

14 See Panos Karnezis, 'An Afternoon Outing,' in *Overheard: Stories to Read Aloud*, ed. Jonathan Taylor (Cromer: Salt, 2012), pp.87–94.

15 As Blake Morrison writes, 'you can trace the idea back to Ancient Greece, where poems would be recited at drinking parties or symposia (often competitively, in a "capping game," one person following another)' (Blake Morrison, 'Why Do Writers Drink?,' in *The Guardian*, 20 July 2013, https://www.theguardian.com/books/2013/jul/20/why-do-writers-drink-alcohol (last accessed 30.4.18)).

and critics have recognised this aspect of the short story: there is a well-known quotation, often attributed to Anton Chekhov, which compares the experience of reading a short story to downing a shot of vodka.[16] Likewise, F. Scott Fitzgerald suggested that 'a short story can be written on a bottle.'[17]

The connection between the narrative structure of drinking and that of the short story can be pursued even further: both drinking and the short story – as the latter has come to be understood since the early twentieth century, and writers such as James Joyce and Katherine Mansfield – often involve some kind of 'epiphany.' 'Early twentieth-century writers,' notes Ailsa Cox, used 'their stories to capture fleeting impressions and changing states of consciousness. Joyce's concept of the "epiphany" – a sudden flash of inner transformation – found its best expression in the short story.'[18] A short story and, say, a night of heavy drinking can equally result in such an epiphany, in the sudden revelation of hidden truths, of long-repressed emotions or memories. Of course, in both cases, the epiphany may be, as Cox puts it, a 'false epiphany'[19] – an illusion, delusion or trick. An epiphany, a 'sudden flash of inner transformation,' in a short story might prove to be just as illusory as a drunken epiphany, in which someone bursts into tears and hugs their friends: 'I love you guys.' Certainly, in Mansfield's famous story 'Bliss' (1918), the main character's epiphanic feeling of 'bliss' is illusory, even delusional. It is, though, a very powerful illusion which dominates most of the story

16 See, for example, Julia Casterton, *Creative Writing: A Practical Guide* (Basingstoke: Palgrave-Macmillan, 2005), p.51, and Paul Curd, 'What is a Short Story?,' in *Thresholds: The International Short Story Forum*, http://thresholds.chi.ac.uk/what-is-a-short-story/ (last accessed 30.4.18).
17 Quoted in Morrison, 'Why Do Writers Drink?'
18 Ailsa Cox, *Writing Short Stories* (Abingdon: Routledge, 2005), p.4.
19 Ibid., p.42.

– and, moreover, it is an illusion which is connected to drunkenness. Early on in the story, the main character bemoans the assumption by an 'idiotic civilisation' that her epiphanic feeling of 'bliss' is necessarily connected to being 'drunk and disorderly.'[20]

However idiotic the connection between epiphanic bliss and drink might seem to her, the link is an ancient one, ingrained in our 'idiotic civilisation' from Ancient Greece onwards. After all, Dionysus was not only the god of wine – of being drunk and disorderly – and the progenitor of literature; he was also the god, significantly enough, of epiphanies. As Hans Oranje notes, 'Dionysus is preeminently the god of epiphany: as god of wine, as god of the Dionysiac festivals, and as the orgiastic god.'[21]

On this mythic level, the modern short story – capturing as it so often does an epiphanic moment – is necessarily connected with both alcohol and Dionysian rites. The short story, it might be claimed, is a Dionysian space, orgy, or rite; or, to put it another way, Dionysus would surely be god of the short story. Like a Dionysian rite, the short story involves, as Cox states, a 'sudden flash of inner transformation,' a 'moment of intense insight, which briefly illuminates the whole of existence,' an 'emotional turning point,' a kind of 'mystical vision … beyond our control.'[22] It can also involve outer transformation, too: the testing and transgression of boundaries (as in 'An Afternoon Outing' and 'On Sunday'), the momentary overturning of hierarchies (as in 'Why Don't You Dance?'), and the defamiliarisation of previous modes of living (as in 'Beers and Poets and Talk'), of ossified relationships (as in 'Bliss'),

20 Katherine Mansfield, 'Bliss,' in *Bliss and Other Stories* (Harmondsworth: Penguin, 1962), pp.95-110, 95.
21 Hans Oranje, *Euripides's Bacchae: The Play and Its Audience* (Leiden: E. J. Brill, 1984), p.100.
22 Cox, *Writing Short Stories*, p.42.

of everyday routines and systems (as in 'On Sunday').

In all these ways, the short story is not only a Dionysian rite: it is also a 'carnivalesque' form, as the Russian critic Mikhail Bakhtin would have understood it.[23] For Bakhtin and others, Earnshaw remarks, 'the festival revels of medieval England ... provided days of misrule when the social world was turned upside down.'[24] Medieval festivals in England and elsewhere were Dionysian rites which saw the 'carnivalesque' suspension of an otherwise-repressive system. As Bakhtin himself puts it:

> the festive liberation of laughter and body was in sharp contrast with the stringencies ... which had preceded or were to follow. The feast was a temporary suspension of the entire official system with all its prohibitions and hierarchic barriers. For a short time, life came out of its usual, legalised and consecrated furrows and entered the sphere of utopian freedom.[25]

Such a 'temporary suspension of the ... official system with all its ... hierarchic barriers' arguably persisted after the Middle Ages, in the miniature, circumscribed, diluted and ambivalent form of the English pub. Obviously, there are all sorts of provisos, caveats and objections to be made in this respect; but, as Earnshaw points out, the English pub does sometimes seem, at least ideally, to represent 'a refuge from authority,' a non-hierarchical space in which 'socially disparate folk'[26] can meet and mingle. The pub represents a partially-carnivalesque space in which people who would not normally meet end up face to face – and interact.

---

23 Mikhail Bakhtin, *Rabelais and His World*, trans. Hélène Iswolsky (Bloomington: Indiana University Press, 1984), p.102.

24 Earnshaw, *The Pub in Literature*, p.8.

25 Bakhtin, *Rabelais and His World*, p.89.

26 Earnshaw, *The Pub in Literature*, pp.8, 18.

The same might be said of the short story: the short story is sometimes a kind of pub in which people from different social classes or contexts, who might otherwise not meet, end up crossing paths and affecting one another. The short story and the pub bring together strangers, testing, defamiliarising and challenging established hierarchies, systems and ways of thinking in carnivalesque moments of misrule, liberation, rebellion, hierarchical overturning. Many short-story writers, in different ways, have recognised and celebrated the 'carnivalesque' element of short stories: the association might be traced back from Angela Carter (in, for example, her collection *Black Venus* (1985)), to Wyndham Lewis (in grotesque parts of *The Wild Body* (1927)) – and from there all the way back to Edgar Allan Poe (in tales such as 'King Pest' (1835), 'Masque of the Red Death' (1842), 'The Cask of Amontillado' (1846) and 'Hop-Frog' (1850)). Many of the stories in this anthology are similarly set in carnivalesque moments of 'misrule,' where hierarchies are temporarily suspended.

This carnivalesque element is no doubt why a great number of short stories, by Mansfield, John Cheever, Joyce and some of the writers here, feature not only pubs, but also dinner parties, festivals, circuses, parties, house parties, cafés, restaurants, and so on. John Cheever's stories, for instance, might seem a long way from Bakhtin's descriptions of medieval popular festivals – but, in bourgeois and displaced forms, there remains something neo-carnivalesque about the drinking, the clash of personalities, the house parties, dances and cafés in stories such as 'Goodbye, My Brother' (1951), 'The Sorrows of Gin' (1953), 'Reunion' (1962), and 'The Swimmer' (1964).[27]

As well as being settings for stories, cafés, house parties and pubs are also contexts in which stories are told – sometimes

27 See John Cheever, *Drinking* (London: Vintage, 2017).

drunkenly. Clearly, the pub is a space in which people share life stories, anecdotes, jokes, tall tales, confessions; as Peter Haining suggests, 'the pub … is somewhere for the telling of stories, tall and otherwise: a platform for the glee-tongued – to use a Belfast expression for those fluent of speech – to spin their yarns.'[28] If this is true of the pub, it is also true of other contexts in which drinking takes place: the consumption of alcohol is often associated with loosening tongues, making speech more fluent (if slurred and potentially incoherent), and yarn-spinning. Again, this association is very old indeed: the ancient Germanic ritual of 'Symbel,' for example, involved toasting and boasting. People would drink mead or ale from a shared drinking horn, and then make speeches or share stories – often competitively.[29] Much more recently, the association between alcohol and yarn-spinning also lies behind the character Rowley Birkin Q.C., in the television comedy series *The Fast Show*: whilst 'very, very drunk' at home, he tells rambling, incoherent stories about being similarly 'very, very drunk' in his past.[30]

If Rowley Birkin's stories are good-humoured and comical, there are also darker connections between excessive alcohol consumption and storytelling. Ever since Thomas De Quincey's *Confessions of an English Opium-Eater* (1821), addiction of various kinds has been seen in terms of a narrative, with a beginning (discovery of the 'drug'), a middle (pleasure and increasing dependence), and an end (pain, horror, sometimes death) – and alcohol addiction is often conceived in these terms. Alcoholism has an in-built narrative or story – or, rather, many stories. This assumption is ingrained in its treatment: the group Alcoholics

---

28 Haining, 'Introduction,' p.14.

29 Thanks to Kristina DeAnn Bell for this reference.

30 See http://www.bbc.co.uk/comedy/fastshow/characters/rowley_birkin.shtml (last accessed 30.4.18).

Anonymous famously encourages sufferers to confess their personal stories about alcohol addiction. In this context, storytelling is seen as powerfully therapeutic; as Laing suggests: 'these anonymous, suffering strangers ... put ... their faith in stories.'[31]

3. Endings: Alcoholic Epiphanies

In particular, this is a faith in *short* stories: alcoholism and its treatment are closer to a short story than they are, perhaps, to a novel. After all, like a short story, alcoholism often involves an 'epiphany' (which might be the first discovery of the 'drug,' or the moment when the alcoholic finally acknowledges his or her addiction); and, again like a short story or collection of short stories, alcohol addiction is often structured around narrative fragments, because excessive alcohol consumption punches holes in memory. 'Alcohol affects the brain in many ways,' writes Laing, 'but one of the most tangible, even to the casual drinker, is the havoc it wreaks on one's ability to recollect the past,' resulting in 'the kind of patchiness of memory ... afflicting [for example] Cheever.'[32]

Many of the authors Laing names in her list of alcoholics (above) were, like Cheever, also well-known short-story writers ('drinkers with short-story problems'). Indeed, the association of short-story writers with alcoholism dates back a long way, almost to the origins of the form: after all, one of the most influential of all formative short-story writers, Poe, was an alcoholic – and maybe set up a pattern for future generations. Arguably, that is, Romantic and post-Romantic writers like Poe and his much-mytholo-

---

31 Laing, *The Trip to Echo Spring*, p.296.
32 Ibid., p.138.

gised life set up 'a series of repeating patterns,'[33] as Laing puts it – 'repeating patterns' which Laing goes on to trace in later writers' lives.

One of these repeating patterns – for short-story writers, poets and novelists alike – is the idea of alcohol as both medicine and poison: for Poe, alcohol famously both drove him on, creatively speaking, *and* destroyed him. He implies as much in one of his last published short stories, 'Hop-Frog,' which might be read as a kind of self-referential alcoholic allegory. The 'Hop-Frog' of the title is a medieval jester who – as many critics have argued – might stand for Poe himself;[34] he has a powerful aversion to wine 'for it excited [him] … almost to madness.'[35] Despite this, the tyrannical king whom he serves – who might stand for a kind of critic – insists that he drink it, believing '"it will brighten [his] … wits,"' so he can come up with an original and imaginative idea for a masquerade ball. Hop-Frog does as he is commanded, and the wine achieves exactly what the king predicts – it brightens Hop-Frog's wits almost to insanity: 'his large eyes gleamed … for the effect of the wine was not more powerful than it was instantaneous.' He is thereafter inspired by the wine and an '"association of idea"' to come up with a '"capital diversion"'[36] for the masquerade ball – one which will mean, ultimately, the horrible death of the king and his ministers, and Hop-Frog's escape.

---

33 Ibid., p.9.
34 'The autobiographical connection is clear,' argues critic Ruth Clements: 'Poe's severe allergic reaction to even a single glass of wine is made manifest in the dwarf Hop-Frog. Wine, Poe tells us, "excites the poor cripple almost to madness"' (Ruth Clements, 'On a Merry-Go-Round Named Denial: Critics, "Hop-Frog," and Poe,' in *Masques, Mysteries and Mastodons: A Poe Miscellany*, ed. Benjamin Fisher (Baltimore: Edgar Allan Poe Society, 2006), pp.145-154, 147; her quotation is from Edgar Allan Poe, 'Hop-Frog,' ' in *Poetry and Tales*, ed. Patrick F. Quinn (New York: Library of America, 1984), pp.899-908, 901).
35 Ibid, p.901.
36 Ibid., pp.901-3.

For Hop-Frog, then, alcohol is both poison and cure: it drives him to insanity, but also helps him come up with a murderous plan of escape. This ambivalent doubleness of alcohol is another repeating pattern across literary history. Like many mind-expanding drugs, alcohol is simultaneously both medicine and poison for the author: it seems to expand horizons, whilst also gradually destroying the faculties – such as coordination, concentration, memory – which are fundamental to writing. As Lewis Hyde writes, alcohol is a 'spirit-helper' which can 'show the novice … the possibility of a different life' (as is the case with Bukowski); it is 'a relaxant and social spirit,' a 'ceremonial spirit,' a 'medicinal, a sedative hypnotic and an anaesthetic'; but at the same time, it is also 'a possessing drug' and seriously 'addictive,' to the point that the alcoholic's very identity is wiped out: 'As a spirit possesses a person he more or less becomes the spirit itself.' Alcohol, according to Hyde, is not only a 'spirit-helper' but also a 'death spirit,' a 'parasite,' a 'poet-killer.'[37]

In this way, alcohol is what philosophers might call the *Pharmakon*: medicine and poison at the same time; and if Hop-Frog is a kind of stand-in for Poe-the-author in the story, it is clear that writing itself is, like alcohol, a kind of *Pharmakon* too. For Poe, alcohol and the writing life were bound together both as ways of living, of sustaining himself (if in markedly divergent senses), *and* as expressions of a powerful drive towards self-destruction. Laing suggests that there is 'a hidden relationship between the two strategies of writing and drinking' because 'both had to do with a feeling that something precious had gone to pieces, and a desire at once to mend it – to give it fitness and shape … – and to deny that it was so.'[38] Writing

37 Lewis Hyde, *Alcohol and Poetry: John Berryman and the Booze Talking* (Dallas: Dallas Institute of Humanities and Culture, 1988), pp.4-5.
38 Laing, *The Trip to Echo Spring*, p.170.

and drinking involve imposing a retrospective narrative or 'fitness and shape' on something 'gone to pieces' – but in doing so, they also involve denial, and a pact with self-destruction. If this is almost literally the case for alcohol abuse, it is also symbolically the case for writing, given that in writing, as the French theorist Roland Barthes famously states, 'the author enters into his own death.'[39] Writing, for Barthes, is deadly for the author. Barthes's compatriot, the philosopher Jacques Derrida, would have understood: in his 1968 essay 'Plato's Pharmacy' (which is almost a weird short story in itself), he talks of writing as both medicine and deadly poison: 'writing is proposed, presented, and asserted as a *Pharmakon*.'[40]

For Alcoholics Anonymous, it is not just writing, but storytelling in general which is a *Pharmakon*: for the AA, as has been seen, alcoholic addiction is a narrative, while the prescribed therapy is also a mode of confessional storytelling. The AA is tapping into a powerful tradition in this respect – a literary tradition which is fully aware of the doubleness of storytelling and alcohol, of their dual roles as the *Pharmakon*. Drinking songs, drinking poems and, indeed, drinking stories have long comprehended this doubleness, this duplicity on the part of alcohol. Even when apparently celebratory, many drinking songs, poems and stories also imply an opposite emotion; even when urging others to drink, drinking songs (for example) often convey a darker sense of desperation, of compulsion, of pessimism. This ambivalence, this doubleness is sometimes unconscious or semi-conscious, sometimes closer to the surface.

---

39 Roland Barthes, 'The Death of the Author,' in *Image, Music, Text*, trans. Stephen Heath (London: Fontana, 1977), pp.142-8, 142.
40 Jacques Derrida, *Dissemination*, trans. Barbara Johnson (Chicago: Univesity of Chicago Press, 1983), p.73.

To give just a few famous examples among thousands: it is certainly close to the surface in John Keats's 'Ode to a Nightingale' (1819), where the narrator asks 'for a draft of vintage! / ... That I might drink, and leave the world unseen,' because he is 'half in love with easeful Death.'[41] In a very different context, the complex association between drinking and death reappears in the 'Alabama Song' (1927) by Elisabeth Hauptmann and Kurt Weill: 'For if we don't find the next whisky bar / I tell you we must die.'[42] The association is similarly explicit in 'Das Trinklied vom Jammer der Erde' ('The Drinking Song of Earth's Sorrow'), the first song in Gustav Mahler's cycle *Das Lied von der Erde* (composed 1908, published 1911), based on translations from Chinese poetry by Hans Bethge:

> The firmament is blue eternally, and the earth
> Will long stand fast and blossom in spring.
> But you, O man, for how long do you live?
> Not for a hundred years can you delight
> In all the rotten trash of this earth!
>
> ... Now take the wine! Now it is time, companions!
> Drain your golden goblets to the dregs!
> Dark is life, and so is death!

In a later song from the same cycle, 'Der Trunkene im Frühling,' ('The Drunkard in Spring'), the singer asks:

---

41 John Keats, 'Ode to a Nightingale,' in *Selected Poems*, ed. John Barnard (London: Penguin, 2007), pp.193-4.
42 Elisabeth Hauptmann, 'Alabama Song,' in *Bertholt Brecht: Poems and Songs From the Plays*, ed. and trans. John Willett (London: Methuen, 1990), p.38.

If life is but a dream
Why then toil and fret?
I drink till I can drink no longer,
The whole livelong day…

I fill my glass again,
And drain it to the dregs…
For what does spring matter to me?
Let me be drunk![43]

Drinking in these two interlinked songs is both hedonistic escape from 'toil and fret,' the 'rotten trash of this
earth,' and an expression of a death drive: implied in the
escapist desire to get away from life's 'toil and fret,' and
'drain [the wine] … to the dregs' is a kind of death-wish.
After all, 'dark is life, and so is death,' so there is little to
choose between them. Both Bethge's and, indeed, Hauptmann's lyrics, in this sense, are deeply nihilistic – a nihilism
shared by many drinking songs and poems.

Despite such nihilism, Bethge's and Hauptmann's lyrics
might bring to mind a much older model, from the Judeo-
Christian tradition: namely, the passage from Isaiah (22:13),
which bears witness to what is, in effect, a kind of Biblical
carnivalesque, a temporary suspension of God's authority:
'And behold joy and gladness, slaying oxen, and killing
sheep, eating flesh, and drinking wine: let us eat and drink;
for tomorrow we shall die.'[44] In all of these texts – Keats,
Bethge, Hauptmann, Isaiah – drinking is simultaneously a
bulwark against death (a way of forgetting that 'tomorrow
we shall die') and an implicit sign of that impending death.
Some poems go further: in Moriya Sen'an's death poem of
1838, death and drinking are transcendentally combined:

43 Quoted in Cooke, *Gustav Mahler*, p.108-9, 112.
44 Isaiah 22:13, in *The Bible: King James Version*.

26

Bury me when I die
beneath a wine barrel
in a tavern.
With luck
The cask will leak.[45]

Drinking, here, is again both an extension of life (an afterlife of drinking) and simultaneously an expression of death.

If this is all true of drinking – as portrayed by Sen'an, Isaiah, and others – something analogous might be said of the short story form, too. The short story form might be said to be 'like' drinking, insofar as it is an expression of life – a description of lived experience – whilst, at the same time, often signifying implicitly or explicitly the death of the characters involved. Many of the stories in this anthology are haunted by death, in various forms; and there are, of course, stories – both within and beyond this anthology – which literally end with the death of one or more of the characters involved. It is a common way to end a story. But perhaps, on a more metaphorical level, the form itself also has a kind of in-built death-wish or death drive. By definition, the short story is often a teleological form: because of its shortness, the short story is often explicitly end-orientated, in a way which is less obvious in longer, more digressive forms, such as the novel. As Dominic Head suggests, 'the short story is that genre in which anticipation of the ending is always present.'[46] Whether or not that narrative ending involves the literal death of one or more of the characters, it is still the case that the short story seeks its

---

45 Quoted in *Japanese Death Poems: Written by Zen Monks and Haiku Poets on the Verge of Death*, ed. Yoel Hoffmann (Tokyo: Tuttle, 1986), p.81. Thanks to Will Buckingham for this reference.

46 Dominic Head, *The Modernist Short Story* (Cambridge: Cambridge University Press, 1992), p.13. Thanks to Hannah Stevens for this reference.

own end – its own self-destruction, as it were – in a much more linear way than, say, the novel or full-length play.

Of course, all forms of narrative imply some kind of death drive; as Nicholas Royle points out, Sigmund Freud's great work *Beyond the Pleasure Principle* (1920) – the work which formulated the notion of an innate 'death drive' – is a 'theory of narrative' as well as one of human psychology. Narratives, according to this theory, have an inherent 'death drive' as much as human beings: 'when it comes to the death drive,' writes Royle,

> every fictional text ... will figure its workings differently ... When it comes to a good story ... we all want the end, but we don't want it right away: we want a story that holds itself up, takes certain kinds of detours, creates certain digressions and postponements. A good story is one that knows it has to end, but ... it has to have "the right death, the right end."[47]

In short stories, though, the '"right death"' and '"right end"' come after much fewer 'digressions and postponements' than a longer work; the end is much closer to the surface in a short story, and is often implied from the beginning. This is particularly the case in Modernist short stories – stories near-contemporaneous with Freud's work – where the 'epiphany' overshadows much of the narrative: in Mansfield's 'Bliss,' the epiphanic ecstasy of the main character dominates most of the text. Likewise, in Fitzgerald's story 'An Alcoholic Case' (1937), the self-destructive death drive of the alcoholic is clear from start to end. The '"right end"' – the alcoholic's death – is indicated from the start, as it is in many short stories, and there are

---

47 Nicholas Royle, *The Uncanny* (Manchester: Manchester University Press, 2003), p.95. He is quoting from Freud's *Beyond the Pleasure Principle*.

very few 'digressions and postponements' along the way. In this sense, then, the short story form has a near-conscious death drive.

Indeed, in many short stories, the death-wish of the form is directly connected to the self-destructive, alcoholic drive of the characters – fusing drinking, ending, and death in ways not unlike Sen'an's death poem. This fusion is suggested in Cheever's story 'The Scarlet Moving Van' (1959), where the alcoholic 'Gee-Gee' seems to have 'heard, from some wilderness of his own, the noise of a distant horn that prophesied the manner and the hour of his death,' as well as 'the agonies of death' for others in the community.[48] The fusion is even more overt in Joel Lane's story 'Without a Name' (2012) in which the main character's self-destructive addiction to a mysterious, poisonous drink called 'Nada' is also a quest for oblivion – for 'Nada' or nothingness – which structures the whole narrative, beginning to inevitable end.[49] Something similar happens in Fitzgerald's story 'An Alcoholic Case': here, the story is propelled forwards by the self-destructive drive of the alcoholic, his 'Will to Die'[50] – a will which ultimately brings about both his death and the near-simultaneous end of the story. The alcoholic's 'Will to Die' and the story's Will to End are coterminous. Moreover, the author himself seems, as Barthes would expect, to 'enter into his own death' in this story, or at least to imagine it, given that the story's fictional alcoholic mirrors his author in various ways: the fictional alcoholic is a kind of writer (a cartoonist), and Fitzgerald was,

---

48 John Cheever, 'The Scarlet Moving Van,' in *Drinking Stories* (London: Vintage, 2017), pp.83-102, 92.

49 Joel Lane, 'Without a Name,' in *Overheard: Stories to Read Aloud*, ed. Jonathan Taylor (Cromer: Salt, 2012), pp.205-10.

50 F. Scott Fitzgerald, 'An Alcoholic Case,' in *The Oxford Book of American Short Stories*, ed. Joyce Carol Oates (Oxford: Oxford University Press, 1992), pp.301-309, 309.

notoriously, a self-destructive alcoholic. For the fictional alcoholic, his real-life counterpart, and the story itself, alcohol is, as Hyde puts it, 'the death threat.'[51]

4. Mixing Drinks: The Stories

That's the problem with drinking, I thought, as I poured myself a drink. If something bad happens you drink in an attempt to forget; if something good happens you drink in order to celebrate; and if nothing happens you drink to make something happen.
– Charles Bukowski, *Women*[52]

You've opened a book that's full of the pleasures and pains of drinking – a book in which eighteen writers explore 'the unspeakable truths'[53] that push us to pour a drink. We'd like you to think of this book as a pub, and each story as a different kind of drinker: the gentle customer at the bar who offers to buy you a drink; the tipsy joker propping up the counter; the gregarious punter spouting alcohol-fuelled pipedreams; the lonely drinker tucked away in a shadowy corner; the self-involved drinker on a downward spiral; the paralytic head-butter, desperate for alcoholic obliteration. And so on.

Reading through the stories will feel a little like getting drunk, as you experience the highs and lows of drink and how its mysterious force sets things in 'relentless motion,'[54]

---

51 Hyde, *Alcohol and Poetry*, p.9.

52 Charles Bukowski, *Women* (London: Virgin Books, 2009), p.176.

53 Morrison, 'Why Do Writers Drink?'

54 Raymond Carver, *Fires: Essays, Poems, Stories* (New York: Vintage Books, 1984), p.26.

in Carver's words. Perhaps this is why we have such a ful-some history of alcoholic writers writing about alcoholic characters. Certainly, it's an ongoing topic of speculation for both writers and critics. Morrison, for instance, con-siders why writers drink and feels there is no simple an-swer; the reasons are manifold: 'From boredom, loneliness, habit, hedonism, lack of self-confidence; as stress relief or a short-cut to euphoria; to bury the past, obliterate the present or escape the future.'[55] Morrison suggests that fic-tion, perhaps, more adequately expresses 'the unspeakable truths.' The addict inhabits an ambivalent space between private gratification and public condemnation, and so we tend to associate dependency with denial and lies. Like-wise, fiction, 'with its beautiful deceptions and its artful lies,'[56] as Will Blythe puts it, is indeed a fitting method to explore the paradoxical power of alcohol.

The writer often starts from experience, from some deep impression or perception of life, but for experience to be of any use the writer must give it distance. Laing's lively article 'The 10 best Books on Literary Drunkenness'[57] ex-plores this process, detailing a telling selection of the most famous books and stories on drinking and booze, by writ-ers Thomas Hardy, Fitzgerald, Rhys, Charles R. Jackson, Kingsley Amis, Williams, Cheever, Hemingway, Berryman and Carver. These writers (all alcoholics, apart from Hardy) have alchemised their own personal misery, humiliations, defeats and delusions into their fictional characters' stories.

55 Morrison, 'Why Do Writers Drink?'

56 Will Blythe, 'Introduction,' in *Why I Write: Thoughts on the Craft of Fiction*, ed. Will Blythe (London: Little, Brown and Company, 1998), pp.xiii-xxv, xxiii.

57 Olivia Laing, 'The 10 Best Books on Literary Drunkenness,' in *Daily Beast*, 28 December 2013,
https://www.thedailybeast.com/the-10-best-books-on-literary-drunkenness (last accessed 14.03.18).

As Laing points out, Carver's story 'Where I'm Calling From' draws on his own experiences with alcohol, and Berryman's novel *Recovery* (1973) is a thinly-veiled fictionalised account of his time in an alcohol treatment centre.

Of course, literary drunks are not conceived solely by alcoholic authors. Hardy and Jane Austen, for example, both highlight the potentials of intoxication. Hardy perfectly captures the unpredictable nature of the alcoholic in *The Mayor of Casterbridge* (1886), a morality tale of a country gentleman who falls on hard times after a series of bad decisions – notably his drunken impulse to sell off his wife and child. And in Austen's novel, *Emma* (1815), alcohol fuels one of the great scenes in which Mr. Elton – drunk and without restraint – leaps into the heroine's coach after a dinner party, to make advances.

Throughout history, writers (alcoholic and sober) have employed the liberating, menacing force of booze in their fiction because it functions to enhance emotion and accelerate plot, creating tensions that shine a shrewd light onto the social and political implications behind inebriation. As in life, alcohol releases characters' inhibitions, enabling them to reveal their dreams and fears. It breaks taboos. It complicates identities and relationships, and can bring lives crashing down in an instant. 'There but for the grace of god …' we can't help but think as we read, fearful and captivated.

The remit for the generous writers contributing to this collection was loose rather than prescriptive, asking for stories that explore the comedies, tragedies, pleasures, pains and horrors of drinking. As editors, we feel that fiction is more telling without imposed agendas, as so much is revealed in those moments writers *choose* to present. The result (we think) is a daring, intimate, entertaining and diverse collection, ranging from gritty realist (historical and contemporary), to memoiristic, through to fantastic stories. The stories shift between the painfully real and darkly comic, and neither glamorise nor seek to moralise the appeal of alcohol. The stories' people – the striving working class and aspiring middle class – are by no means all alcoholics. Rather, we see how alcohol serves as a social prop in the individual's struggle with personal crisis.

The pages are crammed with bewildered, disillusioned, dissatisfied, angry, and hopeful people dealing with the failures of marriage and family, bereavement, trauma and loss (in stories by Melanie Whipman, Karen Stevens, Jonathan Taylor, Alison Moore, David Swann, Bethan Roberts, Sue Wilsea, Jenn Ashworth, Hannah Stevens, Kate North); and a lack of purpose and meaningful connections in personal and professional life (Judith Allnatt, Jane Roberts, Michael Stewart, Cathy Galvin, Desmond Barry, Jane Feaver, Laurie Cusack). The characters' emotional responses to the fracture of human relations, most often seen in a change in family structures, unmask our need for love, understanding and permanence.

The anthology shows that alcoholic beverages are never 'socially neutral.' Each drink brims with symbolic meaning. The dour drinking of whisky and lager in tartan tins is a nationalistic sign of loyalty and identity (Jane Feaver); a proffered bottle of coffee liqueur is a symbolic medium to reinforce shaky familial connections (Alison Moore); the celebratory bottles of Champagne signify the fulfilment of middle-class expectations and aspirations (Melanie Whipman); the pursuit of hedonistic drinking indicates membership in a particular group (Jonathan Taylor, Desmond Barry).

Human beings love ritual, and almost every event with any significance is celebrated with some sort of ceremony. Birth, marriage, death, professional achievement, and Christmas are marked with alcohol (in stories by Melanie Whipman, Jonathan Taylor, Jenn Ashworth, Louis de Bernières, Bethan Roberts). Yet drinking rituals are also used to define less momentous events, such as the transition from work to home, and from work to leisure, or for making it through an arduous day (Michael Stewart, Hannah Stevens, Judith Allnatt, Alison Moore, Sue Wilsea, Laurie Cusack). Indeed, alcohol itself is assessed and celebrated through the ritual of wine tasting (Jane Roberts), and events such as Beaujolais Day (Kate North).

Drinking is essentially a social act and subject to traditions, rules and norms. Together, the stories reveal and illuminate the daily paradoxes and pressures of living in westernised cultures that promote uninhibited consumption alongside social regulation and personal responsibility.

Guy de Maupassant feels that the writer's goal is not to tell a story and entertain, but to make us think and understand 'how minds are modified under the influence of environmental circumstances.'[58] 'Modern life,' Hemingway famously wrote, 'is often a mechanical oppression and liquor is the only mechanical relief.'[59] In these stories, alcohol mediates between the inner and outer lives of people, offering sharp insights into how we relate to, and are affected by, the world around us. Capitalism is known for its dynamism and innovation, but it is also known for its tendency to generate instability through bouts of 'financial crises, job insecurity, and for its failures to include

---

58 Guy de Maupassant, 'The Writer's Goal,' in *The Story and its Writer: An Introduction to Short Fiction*, ed. Ann Charters (New York: Bedford / St. Martins, 2003), p.1533.
59 Postscript to letter to critic, poet and translator Ivan Kashkin, August 19, 1935; published in *Ernest Hemingway: Selected Letters 1917-1961*, ed. Carlos Baker (New York: Granada Publishing, 1981), p.420.

the disadvantaged.'[60]

Many of the stories explore the psychological effects of working within, keeping up with, or reacting against such an economy. We see the loss of ideals and subsequent disillusionment for displaced Irish workers living in fleeting and unstable working communities (Cathy Galvin, Laurie Cusack); lack of personal fulfilment in striving for outward success and social status through work and the workplace (Michael Stewart, Judith Allnatt, Jane Roberts); nostalgic yearning for the Dionysian pleasures of a less 'puritan' economy (Louis de Bernières); the breakdown of familial bonds within a working-class community, divided by prescribed gender roles and expectations (Bethan Roberts); social fragmentation and its effects when individuals choose to opt out of society and its systems (David Swann, Desmond Barry, Laurie Cusack).

The characters here drink to express or mask their fears about the quality of life, and life's unmanageability. And the drink they turn to reveals who they think they are. In *Consuming Life*, Polish sociologist Zygmunt Bauman states that we consume in order to craft and express our identities.[61] In these stories, gender, age, class, status, aspirations and affiliations are frequently expressed through beverage choice: the middle class drink Champagne, fine wine, brandy and whisky; the working class drink plonk, whisky, tinnies and cider. For some, drink and drinking to excess derive from a desire (literal and symbolic) to obliterate one's sense of 'self' (Michael Stewart, Hannah Stevens, Jenn Ashworth, Sue Wilsea, Alison Moore); to revise and reinvent oneself (Judith Allnatt, Kate North); to regress in

---

60 'Theory of Capitalism,' The Centre on Capitalism and Society, Columbia University, http://capitalism.columbia.edu/theory-capitalism (last accessed 02/04/18).

61 Zygmunt Bauman, *Consuming Life* (Cambridge, Polity Press, 2007).

order to capture and express a primitive inner force that is repressed in more 'civilised' society (Desmond Barry, Laurie Cusack).

E. M. Forster felt that characters should exhibit the 'incalculability of life,'[62] and in its capacity for decomposing and recomposing the self, alcohol gets at the heart of life's incalculability. Here, we witness the swift transformations in situation, mood, perception and insight that come from the bottle. We follow people who are in flux, changeable, unpredictable – as Richard Ford puts it, 'rather *un*fixed.'[63] The best short stories offer us something of life's and the self's mystery, their *un*fixedness. As such, these stories invite us to stare into our glass not merely to see ourselves reflected in our drink, but to glimpse other, possible selves as we turn the pages. So pull up a bar stool and order a double. Prepare yourself to meet fellow drinkers.

62 E.M. Forster, *Aspects of the Novel* (London: Penguin, 1974), p.81.
63 Richard Ford, 'The Art of Fiction,' No. 147, *The Paris Review*, Fall 1996, https://www.theparisreview.org/interviews/1365/richard-ford-the-art-of-fiction-no-147-richard-ford (last accessed 26/03/18).

Jackie Kennedy and the Widow
by Jenn Ashworth

12.44pm – two inches of warm white wine left in the bottle from last night.

It goes down in two gulps. She puts the empty bottle back in the fridge and closes it quickly so her mother, who is waiting in the living room, doesn't catch her. She's thirty-two years old and it is past lunchtime. If she wants to drink to get rid of the hangover, she bloody well will. She vows to count her units today, though. There's an app for that somewhere on her phone.

Are you ready, love?

She waits by the fridge, counting the magnets stuck to its door. Souvenirs from holidays they'd spent abroad. Her favourites: a scowling gorilla demanding coffee and a pair of red sparkling shoes. *No place like home.* She fights the urge to sweep them away and imagines the clatter, then her mother on her hands and knees gathering them from the kitchen floor and patiently, without saying a word, putting them back. No ridiculousness allowed. Today is and is not about her.

Come on, love. You can do this.

She has a plan. She's going to be like Jackie Kennedy. She conjures up the pink suit. Her frozen face.

There's a magnet in the shape of a shamrock they'd bought in a gift shop in Galway. Not exactly a honeymoon, though they'd pretended it was. They spent four days in bed, trying to get her pregnant before the chemotherapy would sterilise him. It was unromantic, workmanlike fucking and she'd arrived back home with cystitis, unfertilised.

The car arrives and she gets into it with her parents. The

coffin goes in a different car in front. Her mother gives her a tissue and a mint. Pulls a thread from her sleeve. The journey passes slowly, but she misses everything.

2.36pm – double gin and tonic with ice and lemon.

From her father, who wants to get in there first. The honour of buying the first drink. A duty of his. As if this is a wedding reception or a wetting of the baby's head, except there will be no baby.

Get it down you.

It is a reward for not crying at her own husband's funeral. Or it's medicinal. To warm her up. Thaw her out. To crack her. She won't crack. She's channelling Jackie now, on the aeroplane, hand on her heart and the blood still tacky on her sleeve. She downs the gin in one – two – and lets the glass hit the bar a little too hard. The ice cubes rattle. She wipes her mouth and looks towards the narrow tables of cling-filmed sandwiches and chicken drumsticks.

The guests are waiting for her to say they can eat. Nobody will do anything without her say-so. She must know all of these faces. What would Jackie do? She'd walk stiffly over to the tables to unpeel the cling-film with dignity, rolling the film into little balls of plastic and handing them to her mother.

4.24pm – white wine spritzer.

Pressed into her hand by the vicar, who she doesn't know from Adam. Her mother sorted it. Thought it would be a good idea. To have hymns. Some sense of the beyond. There have been other drinks and she's already swaying slightly as he reaches for her hands and holds them between his.

Vicars should have dry hands. Papery skin, like bibles.

This one is fat and clammy, a bit pissed and his hands are feverish. He says something to her and she tries to look neutral. She pretends a doctor has injected every single muscle in her face with botox and that she's frozen like that: numb and beautiful. She's a sculpture. She's carved from milk. She will nod until the time comes to extract her hands and get another drink.

Every hair on your head has been counted, the vicar is saying, which sounds like a curse. She pulls her hands away and picks up her drink and she must be drunker than she'd intended to get because her mother is at her arm then, pulling it gently.

A plate of sandwiches appears. Tuna and mayonnaise. A mini pork pie, cut into quarters.

Eat, her mother says. *You must eat.*

4.46pm – white wine (large)

He couldn't eat, not at all, towards the end. First there were protein shakes and liquid meals and bottles of coke. She measured the powders and fluids and counted every calorie. Then there were bowls of ice cream and melted chocolate coating the backs of teaspoons. And then there was nothing, and he wasted. There's all the food anyone could want here. She doesn't know who is paying for all this or who placed the order. His father?

The hard-core friends are still seated at one table – her friends, mainly, as his drifted away when he got ugly and stopped talking. They nod when she passes and push drinks into her hands.

Lovely service. Lovely service.

At another table sits family – hers and his. Sitting together and chatting as if they are at a wedding. Will everyone stay and keep on mentioning *the lovely service* until she leaves?

Will everyone keep saying that until she's had enough and skips out?

She's single now. Two months ago she shagged a guy she'd met in a nightclub and wasn't sure what to do with her wedding ring. She'd soaped it off in his bathroom and ended up leaving it there. Are her mother and his father talking about her lack of wedding ring? Fuck them. There's a glass in front of her and she presumes it is hers.

5.20pm – whisky (double – make unknown)

The short glass is in her hand. She holds onto it tightly and takes it with her into the toilet. Balances it on the top of the cistern while she pisses. Lets her head droop forward onto her knees. She could sleep here. She could sleep. There hasn't been proper sleep for months. Dozing in chairs at the hospice during the day and half the night. Prowling bars and clubs in the small hours. Catching her reflection in a taxi window in the morning's half-light and not quite recognising what she sees.

He was always good on a hangover. That's what she said about him, when nine years ago her friends asked her about this new man she was seeing. *He's good on a hangover.* He'd make toast and milky coffee and bring it to her bed, standing there naked, despite the open bedroom curtains.

Somebody overdid it last night, he'd say. And she, without an ounce of shame, spread-eagled across the sheets in the syrupy glare of the morning sunshine, could only smile. That's how it was. He never made her feel like she was bad, even though he knew her so well he must have known that she was not a good person.

She stands. Wipes. Wriggles the skirt back into place then sits back on the closed lid, nursing the whisky. She doesn't even like whisky.

Perhaps a cup of tea? her mother had said, and she'd fled in here, avoiding the mirrors. The door to the toilets opens and closes.

You all right in there? Not flushed yourself away?

A male voice. Her heart lifts and dips and now she is near to crying, though she only coughs. She finishes the whisky and manages to say, *I'm still here.*

5.24pm – tap water

It's his brother. She unlocks the door and he's holding a glass of iced tap water out to her. She takes it but does not drink. He looks around, perhaps baffled at his surroundings: the ladies' bogs. There's a poster on the wall about taking care of your drinks so you don't get spiked.

Do you want me to call you a cab?

She shakes her head, takes the water and pours it down the sink. She feels his attention on the side of her neck, like a hand. His name is Daniel and he never visited the hospice. *Does my head in to see him like that*, he'd said, just once. She collected that phrase and held it close and treasured it through all the hours she did her own head in, sitting there, counting her husband's breaths and cleaning his mouth with tiny pink sponges on sticks.

His mother had tried to explain: *Wants to remember his brother as he was.* As if memory was a stream of water that shouldn't be polluted. That's what it says above the taps. A little red sign in old-fashioned type. *Non-potable water.*

She looks at the empty glass. That was foolish and ill-mannered, pouring it away like that. Jackie would have taken it and sipped her water whilst shaking hands and kissing cheeks. Every time someone said, *Wasn't it a lovely service?* she would have said, *Oh yes, it was a great comfort*, or, *The vicar had a sense of what he meant to all of us, didn't he?* Jackie was a politician's wife and for a while she was the most photographed woman in the world: caught in the attentive glare of a thousand flashbulbs. Jackie could be a good person because everyone was always watching. She, on the other hand, is just a primary school teacher who has been on leave for a whole term and she has nothing at all to say, so instead she has poured the water away. The empty glass sits on the edge of the sink.

Danny is flushed and trembling and he doesn't say *that was a nice service* or *at least he's out of his suffering now* but he comes towards her, and there are his arms and his suit jacket is too small for him and smells like aftershave and dry cleaning. She leans forwards, out of her heels. The hug turns into a kiss that is wet and unpleasant. She feels his teeth. They're in the cubicle now, her back against the un-locked door, one foot on the pan.

From very far away she sees herself, the rabbity bumping of their hips, and he's crying, and nobody is having a good time.

6.29pm – various

In the middle of a conversation with her mother-in-law (does she still have a mother-in-law? Does she still count as family?) she realises she is laughing, very loudly. She presumes, slowly, that she must have just been told a joke. As her laugh dies away she thinks this is unlikely.

I'm actually just going to step outside and take a breath of fresh air, she says, and there are offers – his mother, hers, a friend or two still taking advantage of the remnants of buffet and bar – to come with her. She waves them away. The door to the pub opens with a struggle – she pulls when she should have pushed, then pushes too hard and erupts into the carpark.

It's cold outside. Bracing. The pub is called Sea View or Sea's Rest or something like that. She views a carpark and a dual carriageway and a street into a housing estate and can't even smell the sea. The clouds are low but the sun is breaking through and casting strange, harsh shadows on the tarmac. She's not drunk at all now. This is the second wind, where drunkenness gives way to an urgent kind of clarity. There's a buzzing in her limbs. She could run. She could do star jumps. Her blood thrums inside her head. She pictures all her vessels filled with light. Perhaps some-one's slipped her something. No. She sits at a wooden pic-nic table and necks whatever it is that's left in a trio of abandoned glasses. She fancies a cigarette. There's a shop in the housing estate: she's almost certain of it.

9.48pm – double gin and tonic

Jackie would never bail out on the wake in favour of a solo-pub crawl. Wake for one. The last time she checked her mobile phone there were fifteen missed calls. It buzzes in her pocket again and she turns it off. Scans the bar, which is full of unpromising men. She is not exactly on the prowl, but willing. *Open to possibility*, she will say, if anyone asks. Open to the possibility of feeling better. Of feeling some-thing, anyway.

She gulps her drink and neatly vomits between two bar stools. The liquid is clear, slightly foamy. She regards the puddle curiously for a moment then leaves as the barman approaches to throw her out. There's a look of disgust on his face. He has her down for some ordinary drunk.

I've just been at a funeral, she says, over her shoulder. What she means is *all bets are off*, and *I need to find the worst thing possible, and do it right away*, and then she remembers that she has already done this. She meanders towards the next pub – *but who will know me now?* The night is black and orange and red and green; the city centre dark and studded with traffic lights.

10.46pm – double gin and tonic

There's a man here talking about his favourite books. He's shouting because the music is bone-shakingly loud and asking her – she thinks he is asking her – if she reads. He is talking about *Papillion* and asking if she's ever read it and telling her that this single book – which he read when he was inside on a medium stint for armed robbery – has changed his entire life. She doesn't think he's hitting on her. She's no idea where she is, only that it's the sort of place where the lights give everything white – the lint on the man's blue tee-shirt, his teeth, the whites of his eyes – a strange kind of glow.

She stands on tiptoes and holds his face between both hands. She wants to tell him how special he is. How important. He must not let his past hold him back. She kisses him full on the lips and he laughs but doesn't stop her, and she carries on talking, stumbling over the word 'prejudice.' She tries to get him to dance. One of his friends holds up the lit oblong of his mobile, perhaps to film them. She takes his hands to pull him towards the dance floor. When he won't come, she takes offence and leaves the club.

She slips and hurts her ankle as she picks her way down the stairs from the door of the club and into the street. Nobody notices. Her phone is missing, but it was only a cheap one and it doesn't matter. The hospice will not be phoning her tonight.

The town flickers past her. Lights. The road lurches, the kerb twisting to catch the heel of her shoe. She drops the bottle and it shatters on the pavement. This draws attention: a cheer comes up behind her – *more men*, she thinks – but she does not turn. Doesn't smile and tag along with them. Does not ask them for a cigarette. She carries on walking. The uneven sound of her heels is comforting. Then there's pain, though not much, in her hands. The pavement rears upwards and knocks her cheekbone, but she gets up again quickly.

Now she does cry, because she's lost and can't remember where the taxi-rank is and all her words have flown away from her. She counts her steps. The entire world has diminished to this: one foot in front of the other, unsteady, but still going. One. Two. Three. If she keeps doing this, she will get somewhere. Daniel's face appears – he won't meet her eye – then floats away. There's a nasty website where people post mobile phone pictures of drunk women pissing in bus stops, or fucking in alleys, or unconscious against lampposts, their laps covered in vomit. Jackie would never end up on a website like that. She just wouldn't.

You're home safe, that's the main thing, he'd say. Even though she no longer told him what she got up to on her night-time adventures, he was still always good on a hangover. Even after chemo, when he was too sick to bring her the coffee. He would make room for her in bed and let her choose a film to watch on Netflix. She swigged his Oromorph out of the bottle and made him promise not to tell the nurse.

You've nothing to be ashamed of, he said once. Only once. That was in Galway, when she'd tripped and skinned her knees on the way back to the hotel. She'd cried then. Back in their room, he'd been too worried and tired to get it up, and she'd drunkenly shouted that he should make more effort because this was their last chance, and didn't he realise they'd been here for three days already and the chemo was going to start soon? She had all the appointments, the three-month-cycles, marked up on a special calendar. There were reminders on her mobile phone. Ovulation. Consultants. Scans.

Eventually, she finds the main street and follows it downhill, towards the park and the river where it will be dark and quiet. She counts her steps until the memories leave her and the town centre street lights fade. She can't hear the river, but she can smell it. She leaves the path. Her heels sink into the wet grass. It is so dark. Nobody will see her here.

4.24am –

She wakes on a bench, her jacket damp because the dew has settled on her as she slept. It is light. She finds her shoes and looks around herself. The light sparks from everything; each drop of water on every blade of grass glows. It hurts, all of it. She vomits. Wipes her mouth. Dry heaves. The hangover hasn't arrived yet, but it is in the post and she could still outrun it. Get home before it hits. Get back to bed and milky coffee and the place where she is known.

Mornings always do this to her: his death comes as news again each dawn.

She vomits, and there is nobody here to take a photograph of her and put it on a nasty website, or to wonder where she's been in her smart black office clothes. Nobody here to ask her what she thought of the service, or to offer her coffee or ask if she wants somebody to call a cab for her.

The early morning light is as sharp as flashbulbs, and as

she leaves the park – still swaying, limping slightly – she feels in her pocket for her phone and keys and finds she has neither. But the day is warming up already and she doesn't cry. Jackie wouldn't cry. They took photographs of her always. There was always someone watching. The sun rises slowly on all of this.

Under the Skin

by Judith Allnatt

Madeleine King had got her face done. Small amounts of botulism toxin had been injected above her eyebrows, below her cheekbones and along the lines that ran from nose to chin on either side of her mouth. 'The substance will cause the muscle to relax,' explained the consultant. 'The area will appear smoother and firmer within a couple of weeks.' Madeleine had given him her hundred-watt smile. 'Well, it has to be done. I'm in PR and I can't mount a charm offensive looking *haggard*,' she'd said, with the tongue-in-cheek self-deprecation that always played so well with her male clients.

Madeleine had liked the consultant; she had felt reassured by his deadpan expression as he drew blue dots on her face to illustrate the areas for attention. He had explained gently that it was not possible to inject directly under the eye, as the skin was too delicate. 'Only the thickness of a rose petal,' he'd added whimsically. She'd thought, well never mind, laughter lines are all right, they're characterful, and imagined her new face as fresher, clearer, but with a hint of maturity and good humour. A rose captured at its prime, in the instant before it blows over.

Nothing had prepared her for the bruising. Now she was home she lay prone on the sofa, trying to bear the mask of pain that was her face. The doctor had said, 'No alcohol with the painkillers,' but this was hell. She checked her watch. Two hours since she'd taken them. Surely she deserved a teensy-weensy drink? She sat up slowly, felt around at the side of the settee and unearthed a bottle of Chivas Regal. She poured some into her medicine glass – only a couple of fingers – for its analgesic properties. She sipped. Winced. Saw it off. Carefully she lowered herself down again and as the warmth stole through her, tried to relax her features into a more placid expression. It wasn't as bad if she kept absolutely still. She imagined herself as a sarcophagus, a painted princess, wooden and immobile.

Her phone rang and she felt around on the coffee table without risking turning towards it. 'Shit,' she muttered, as the bottle of painkillers rattled to the floor. 'Who is it?'

'Hi, it's me.' Marcia sounded much too loud. She was shouting over a background of saxophone, and a foreground of talk and chinking glasses.

A long lunch at the Backstage Bar, thought Madeleine.

'Are you there?' said Marcia.

'Yes,' she said testily.

'Listen. I can do your lunches until Thursday, then we need you back to meet with Charles. He's hinting that he'll find another agency. He doesn't like the creative work on the ad.'

'I can't. I really can't. I look like some kind of *retard*.'

She heard Marcia take a deep breath. 'It's got to be you, hon. You're the one with the "special relationship." Just be there on Friday, even if you look like the Elephant Man.'

The phone went dead. Marcia was supposed to be a friend. I guess I can't expect flowers, Madeleine thought, since all this is self-inflicted. Nonetheless she felt neglected.

Gingerly she got up and made herself some warm milk. Friday! She'd thought she'd be off until Monday at least. She tipped in a slug of brandy and drank it slowly through a straw. The glow put a bit of heart into her and she began to tackle the problem of Friday and Charles. Sunglasses and concealer were probably the answer. If they lunched at *La Vie* they could sit out on the decking and then sunglasses and a floppy hat would look quite natural.

She checked her wardrobe to be sure her cream shift dress

had been dry-cleaned. Charles was always saying how he liked a woman to look pretty. 'Feminine,' he would say in a wistful tone, as though to imply his wife was some kind of lump in gardening gloves. They always drank a lot over lunch. Then Charles inevitably insisted they share a cab and sat too close to her, which Madeleine had learned was her cue to place her handbag on her knees.

'Still,' she consoled herself, 'the wine list is respectable. And it's always good to milk some extra business out of Charles.'

She squashed down firmly her mother's recent comments, which had included phrases like 'waste of life,' and 'glorified hostess,' and had been topped off with, 'If you mix with skunks, don't be surprised if the smell rubs off.' The trouble with my mother, she thought, is her Methodist upbringing. Life doesn't have to be so *serious,* it's so ... unsophisticated. Then with a satisfaction only slightly tinged with guilt – I've moved on from my mother.

On an impulse she went online and ordered herself a large bouquet of Arum lilies, specifying that they should be left by the front door, in water, and that on no account was anyone to ring the bell. They would look good on the hall table, simple and uncluttered. Those smooth petals. Perfect.

Her forehead and cheeks were throbbing again. She dabbed at them gently with a cold flannel and tried to still the murmuring of misgivings. Could this level of pain be normal?

'Of course, it is possible to overtreat an area,' the surgeon had said. And when she'd pressed him he'd added, 'Overtreatment can result in the muscle going into spasm.'

'What, you mean as if it's completely frozen? It won't move?'

'It would be extremely rare,' he had tutted soothingly, 'and I'm very, very careful with my ladies.' Then he had massaged her brow gently towards her hairline, as if to smooth away any suggestion of the puckering of a worry.

Feeling light-headed, she went back to the sofa and dragged a throw around herself. She stared at what was left in the whisky bottle. Two o'clock. If she could get to half past, the pills should surely be out of her system and she'd deserve to finish it off. Then she'd see what else was left in the cupboards and work through it until her face went numb. She flicked on the TV and channel-hopped through a quiz show and adverts for Miracle-gro and stair lifts. Glad to be distracted, she was mildly amused by the obvious difference in target audience that came with day-time viewing. 'Gross,' she murmured as a man enthused about denture fixative.

Changing channel again, she caught the news and was arrested by the image on the screen.

An African child lolled back across its mother's arms, flesh to naked flesh. It was impossible to tell its sex. The skin sagged like stretched latex where muscles and tendons should have shown, and moulded itself painfully over the knobbles of knee and elbow joints. The child's cheeks were sucked into deep hollows, and the closed eyelids seemed strangely flattened. The shot remained focused in this way, showing only the mother's long, elegant hands and flattened breasts, as if, in deference, the cameraman had avoided her grieving face. The reporter explained that in desperation people had eaten the treated grain meant for seed corn. The child was plainly dying.

A cold, sick feeling spread through Madeleine. She touched her fingertips to her swollen mouth, which re-fused to turn downward, and then her brow, which was set as smooth and flat as marble. She imagined her eyes fixed forever in an expression of intelligent amusement, her face frozen in a beautiful, pitiless smile.

In Vino, Vanitas

by Jane Roberts

London. Day 13: Blind Red Tasting.

Close your eyes. Turn off your senses for the final time. Block out everything extraneous. Sight. Smell. Noise. Recalibrate. Now open your eyes.

What can you see?

Here you are in the clinical white room seated at your table once more. You are one of thirty tasters, lined up regiment-style – six by five. Over the preceding twelve days hundreds of bottles have been opened: all twelve days spent at the same table in this white room, going through the same hackneyed processes. At the end of each day – maybe every day of your career – the tasting room reminds you of a preliminary sketch for a Dutch Masters' Vanitas still-life: all youth and harvest drained; faded, pink tracks of once-red wine cascading like tears into the core of empty glasses. Vanitas – the emptiness of a wine glass and its critic … You need a change of scene.

Keep it together. You are a professional.

In front of you is one glass. The last glass. Inspect it. One third full. Pinch the stem between your index finger and thumb of your right hand. Tilt the stem and bowl away from you. Let the wine see the light.

Note: the wine is unfiltered. Tiny particles – phenolic compounds from the grape skins – are suspended – just – in the fluid and shimmer under the stark lighting of the tasting room. At the base of the bowl the remainder of the particles gather as sediment. A faint spectre of a doppelgänger glass and red liquid are projected onto the white table cloth. The wine is clear, not turbid. Not hazy at all.

Tilt the glass further away to a 45-degree angle. Examine the core of the wine.

Note: the opacity is too great to see your thumb on the other side of the glass. Look to the edge of the wine – the viscous rim – where its colour spectrum will be displayed. Previous intensity of the red pigmentation of tannins gives way to … a hint of brown. The 'bricking on the rim' of a mature wine. A few years past its best? Possible effects of oxidation after opening?

Sway the glass – back and forth and left to right – in reverent slow motion, like a holy woman by the altar making the sign of the cross whilst cradling Christ's blood. This table is your altar. The grape is your religion – so wedded are you to your career. Continue to sway the glass. You catch a glimpse of your reflection. Let the wine rest for a moment, count the wrinkles around your eyes. The curvature of the bowl makes your face appear simultaneously bulbous, wizened, two-nosed, then one-eyed, lips full, lips thin: a Picasso-esque jumble of aging womanhood.

The colour of the wine: garnet. The stone on the engagement ring – inherited from your grandmother – that you wear on your wedding-ring finger.

Swirl the wine in the glass – anticlockwise – to turn back time on those wrinkles you saw in your reflection. Raise the glass to your nostrils. Inhale. Deeply.

What can you identify?

Primary aromas: clean and floral – mulberry – dark cherries – wet stones.

Secondary aromas: the milkiness of malolactic fermentation, the vanilla of oak barrelling.

Tertiary aromas: aged in barrels and bottles. Earth. Leather. Mushroom. Brett? Those Brettanomyces yeast characteristics, which account for the savoury elements. Not unpleasant, but developed.

Swill the wine in high tidal waves around the glass to aerate it. Stop. Bring the glass to your mouth, sipping the fluid through slightly pursed lips, allowing a brief intake of air to further enhance the flavour profile on your palate. The garnet liquid hits the tip of your tongue with a sweet rush, strokes its sides with acidity, and unloads a cloying astringency, puckering the sensory papillae at back of the tongue. Drench the inside of your mouth and let the vapours elevate up into your nasal cavity.

What can you taste?

Note: ripe, dark cherry fruits, kirsch-like in their potency. Warm liquorice and pepper zing. A scorched earth-driven character, clad with leather, game meats, and exotic spice. The smoky tannic and heated complexities of two hefty varietals embracing – vying with – a third grape: a softer, more delicate varietal – strawberry and Herbes de Provence, less alcoholic, and ripened at lower sugar levels. The combined finish is full-bodied in texture, with a lingering, dangerous burst of alcohol.

Feel your pulse quicken. Detect a beat that was not present before.

Try to drown out the rhythm with logic. It is not real, this enchantment – that pierces your concentration – that deceives you into imagining your body as a trunk of a vine: a trunk that splits off into cordons, the cordons splitting off into spurs, the spurs blossoming with promising buds, buds flowering, flowers fertilizing, fruit growing green and hard – maturing into succulence. Already you can almost feel tendrils sprouting. Tendrils making you strong and upright. But you know this growth is impossible. Hopeless.

Stop.

Place your glass back on the table. Hands on the white tablecloth. Your mouth waters with acidity. Get ready to spit into the stainless steel bucket to your side. The tannins in the wine have another plan and begin to interact with salivary proteins, bonding your tongue to the arch of your mouth, gluing your lips together.

Close your eyes. Open your eyes. Where are you?

You are in the morgue-white tasting room. And yet … And yet still you sense tendrils sprouting forth from your skin, tendrils yearning to scale the white walls to where the sunlight ganders through the skylight in the ceiling.

Kick off your shoes. Unwind. Stretch your arches. Try to dig your toes past the cool slate tiles, and feel your roots splaying out, labyrinthine explorations for mineral-rich soil strata, tunnelling ever-deeper underground.

Close your eyes.

Smell the earth. Enjoy the heat of the sun leeching into the large galet rocks around the base of your trunk. The Mistral caresses your blossom. The air is purified. Natural. Feel your leaves unfurl and fish for the sun's rays with their chlorophyll nets. You are heavy with fecundity, with clusters of jet-black grapes. Draw up water from the sandstone-mixed soil. You are full. Ripe again.

Open your eyes.

You are Vitis Vinifera.

May Day
by Alison Moore

His tyres rumbled for hours down grey roads that went on and on, year after year. It became soporific. The journey ended in the carpark beneath the Parisian street on which his ex-wife and daughter now lived. He locked the car and walked to Lionel's flat, where he rang the doorbell and waited.

Lionel came to the door, smelling of his Gauloises cigarettes. 'Gareth,' he said. He made it sound like 'garret,' like somewhere lonely and draughty. When Gareth had to say Lionel's name, he said it the English way. Caroline always said it the French way, and Gareth could tell that she enjoyed the feel of the word in her mouth. 'Have you had a good journey?' he asked.

'Not too bad,' said Gareth, coming into the hallway with his weekend bag and a bottle of coffee liqueur, a gift, which Lionel took. They went into the kitchen, where Caroline air kissed Gareth with a paring knife in her hand.

'Rebecca will be home soon,' said Lionel, 'and dinner's on the way. Come with me.'

He led Gareth into the living room, offering him an armchair and taking for himself a place on the two-seater sofa, next to Caroline's knitting. Lionel lit up a cigarette and offered one to Gareth. Gareth held up his hands in refusal. He must look, he thought, like a man surrendering. 'I'll take a drink, though,' he said.

Lionel blew smoke out of his nostrils. He got up and went to a drinks cabinet in the corner of the room. Gareth could not imagine how they managed always to keep it stocked, when he himself was unable to open a bottle of whisky without finishing it before bedtime.

'Same as usual?' asked Lionel.

Gareth nodded. He watched the whisky being poured; he did not need it watered down as Lionel did, or mixed with Caroline's ginger ale. The glass was in his hand when he heard the door to the flat open and close. He heard an exchange in the hallway between Caroline and his daughter, and after a while Rebecca sloped into view. She looked so tall, this long-limbed, long-haired girl; she looked like a teenager, which at twelve she nearly was. He must not tell her that she had grown; she hated that.

'Hi, Dad,' she said, coming into the living room.

'Rebecca,' said Lionel, beckoning her over to where he sat. They exchanged a greeting that was part embrace and part kiss, and Gareth found it hard to watch. It was one of the first things that he had noticed about Lionel: how *tactile* he was.

Rebecca turned to Gareth, who put his glass down empty on a side table. It had been so easy to cuddle her when she was little, but at some point that had stopped. She approached, kissed the space on either side of him, and moved away again. Tomorrow, the two of them would get out of Lionel's flat, where it was impossible to relax; he and Rebecca would have all day together, without Lionel always being there. He imagined them walking arm in arm beside the Seine, and sitting in a café; he would buy a bottle of Burgundy and give Rebecca her first taste of wine.

'I wanted to go to the catacombs,' said Rebecca.

Gareth bowed his head. 'I know,' he said. It had been his idea in the first place, to explore the city's subterranean ossuaries. Foolishly, he had made his daughter a promise that he now found he could not keep. 'The thing is, it turns out, it's closed on Sunday and Monday, and I have to drive home on Tuesday. I have to get back to work.'

'You said it was open on Sunday,' said Rebecca.

'Yes,' said Gareth, 'it normally is, but not on the first of May.' The information was right there on the website, but he had not seen it, or had not understood; it was all in French.

'So the two days you're here, it's closed,' said Rebecca.

'I'm sorry,' said Gareth, 'but we'll do something else.'

Rebecca rolled her eyes.

'You can see a video of the catacombs on the Internet,' he said. He had seen it; he had seen the walls of skulls.

'That's hardly the same,' said Rebecca.

'I know,' said Gareth.

'What *are* we going to do tomorrow, then?' asked Rebecca.

'Well,' said Gareth, 'I thought we could go down the sewers.'

'The *sewers*?'

'Yes,' said Gareth. 'The sewer system is a network of underground tunnels, just like the catacombs, but the sewers are even older.'

'And they stink,' said Rebecca.

Caroline called from the kitchen, 'Rebecca, go and wash your hands before dinner.'

Rebecca made a face but Lionel said, 'Now, Rebecca,' and Rebecca went to wash her hands.

'Please excuse me,' said Lionel. He left the room, turning towards the kitchen, where Gareth imagined him putting his hands on Caroline, speaking to her in French, and she would understand him, smile at him, give him something to carry.

Gareth took his glass over to the drinks cabinet and poured himself a generous measure.

Lionel stood at the head of the table, carving the meat while everyone watched. Caroline had put on some music, much of which Gareth did not recognise, and what he did recognise he did not remember her ever having listened to before. The Bee Gees came on, and Caroline said that her favourite was Barry Gibb, and that she had always preferred him with a beard. 'I do like a man with a beard,' she said, and Lionel stroked his goatee.

A bottle of red wine was already open on the table, and Lionel poured out three glasses. He raised his – 'To family …' – and they drank, and then Lionel passed his glass to Rebecca so that she could have a taste. He turned to Gareth and asked, 'Are you still scuba-diving?'

Gareth said that he was.

'But only in the Thames,' said Lionel.

'I like the Thames,' said Gareth.

Caroline used to say to him, after a Thames Estuary dive, 'You smell of the river.' She meant it in a bad way but Gareth loved the river and was addicted to its cold briny tang.

He detailed his most recent wreck dive and told the story about Henry IV's coffin, which was on its way down the Thames to Canterbury Cathedral when a storm broke and the body was thrown overboard.

'You told this story before,' said Lionel. 'I don't think it's true.'

'Whether he's under the Thames or sealed in a tomb, he's dead either way,' said Rebecca.

Most of Gareth's dives had been shallow, under thirty metres, but recently he had started going deeper. There was a table in his diving manual that showed the effects of nitrogen narcosis on the diver, which began as soon as the diver started his descent and which increased with depth. Even at twenty metres, the diver had mildly impaired reasoning. The diver did not notice it, himself. Or perhaps he was aware of something, like a softening of the senses. It was restful down there. At thirty metres, the diver began to make errors of calculation, and below fifty metres, euphoria could turn into hysterical laughter and terror, before giving way to hallucinations. Well, he had never been that far down, but he had got down to forty-two metres. You had to keep your eye on your depth gauge or the temptation was to keep going deeper.

'I would not like it,' said Lionel. 'I would feel claustrophobic, in that mask you have to wear, and with all those tonnes of water on top of you, and it must get dark down there.'

'It does,' said Gareth. He had been on dives where it was hard to see anything except for the blackness of the water itself. It was disorienting. You could feel disconnected; you could feel peaceful. It was essentially sensory deprivation, as used in both therapy and torture.

'We prefer tennis,' said Lionel, throwing a smile in Caroline's direction. 'It keeps us young.'

Gareth ran a hand over his head, over the inches where his hair used to be. He felt like a monk.

'Who is caring for your dog while you are here?' asked Lionel.

'He died,' said Gareth. 'He had a tumour.'

'He *died*?' said Rebecca.

'You can't just announce something like that,' said Caroline, 'over the dinner table with no warning.'

Rebecca was crying.

'It's surprising, actually,' said Gareth, 'what can be announced over the dinner table with no warning.' He reached for the wine bottle, refilled his glass and ate in silence while Caroline comforted their daughter.

He woke feeling anxious, with a racing heart and clammy skin. He felt as if his brain had shrunk; deep within the walls of his skull, he could feel it pulsing.

He was on the short sofa, in a sleeping bag. The curtains were closed but there were gaps through which he could see daylight.

His wine glass was still there on a side table. He raised himself up on his elbows, picked up his glass and drained the dregs.

He lay down again, wanting to go back to sleep. He tried to get comfortable on Lionel's sofa but was unable to make himself fit. He kept sliding off.

His bladder eventually forced him to get up. He unzipped his sleeping bag and made his way into the hallway. Across from the living room, through an open door, he could see the master bedroom, which reeked of Lionel's Gauloises. He saw the dishevelled bed.

In the bathroom, Gareth pissed and showered but did not shave. He emerged just as Caroline was leaving for work. Standing in the hallway with her coat already on, she looked at his face. Frowning at his chin, she said, 'Do you need me to pick you up a razor?'

Gareth touched his stubble and said no, he had a razor with him.

'All right,' said Caroline, turning away, patting her pockets to see that she had everything she needed. When the door closed behind her, Gareth headed towards the kitchen; he could hear his daughter's voice and paused outside, listening.

'I wanted to go to the catacombs,' she said.

'I know you did,' said Lionel. 'I will take you there.'

'The sewers!' Rebecca said. 'Why would he take me to the sewers?'

Gareth heard Lionel laughing. He entered the kitchen. The two of them were at the breakfast bar – Rebecca had her back to him, but Lionel saw him and asked, 'How did you sleep?'

Gareth rubbed his face and made a non-committal noise.

Lionel poured him a cup of coffee and gestured towards the breakfast items laid out on the counter. 'Everything is here. You can help yourself,' he said as he left the room. Rebecca reached for the jam, and Gareth watched her spreading her circles of toasted baguette.

He said, 'I've got a riddle for you.' Rebecca had always liked riddles when she was little. 'I never was, am always to be; no-one ever saw me, nor ever will. What am I?'

Rebecca pointed to her mouth, which she had just filled, to indicate that she could not talk to him. Lionel came back into the kitchen. He said to Gareth, 'Do you need to borrow my razor?'

'I have a razor,' said Gareth.

'Are you trying to grow a beard?' asked Lionel. 'When you dive, it will interfere with the seal on your mask. Your mask will leak.'

Rebecca stood up, still chewing, and put her plate into the sink.

'You look tired,' said Lionel, observing Gareth.

Through the last of the food in her mouth, Rebecca said, 'We can just stay in, if you're tired.'

'I'm not tired,' said Gareth.

'You *look* tired,' said Rebecca.

'We can watch a film,' said Lionel. A *feelm*. He made a few suggestions to Rebecca, to which she responded enthusiastically.

'We can watch a film this evening, Rebecca,' said Gareth, 'but I wanted to spend today doing something together.'

'We can watch a film *together*,' said Rebecca.

Gareth could not stress in front of Lionel that his plans for the day had not included him. 'We don't have to go to the sewers,' he said. 'We could just go for a walk by the river.'

'Maybe next time,' said Rebecca, who was already going with Lionel into the living room.

With one hand clutching his untouched cup of coffee and the other scratching at his itchy stubble, Gareth said quietly to himself, 'Tomorrow. I'm tomorrow.' He looked at the coffee liqueur that he had brought to give to Caroline, and which Lionel had taken from him; it was out on the counter, not yet opened. Gareth took a slug of his coffee, unscrewed the cap and topped up his cup. He went through to the living room, where the film was already playing. Rebecca was on the two-seater sofa; Lionel was sitting beside her, holding the remote control.

Gareth sat down in the armchair, but he found that he could not follow the film – he was distracted by Lionel, who laughed too often and too loudly. Gareth returned to the kitchen for more coffee, and before the film was half-way through, he had left the flat.

He walked in the direction of the Seine and then took the metro to Pont de l'Alma, the stop for the sewers. He was not far from the Eiffel Tower. A few years before, he had taken Rebecca up the Eiffel Tower, or part of the way up. The structure was never meant to be permanent, he had told her; it was always supposed to be temporary, but it had been standing strong, this wrought iron tower, for well over a century now.

'I know,' she had said, sounding like a teenager even then. 'I live here, remember?'

On the first level of the Eiffel Tower, there was a glass floor, on which they stood, looking down at the ground below, and Gareth, with a little bounce, said, 'I hope it's strong.' On the second level, they joined the snaking queue for the lift that would take them to the very top. After shuffling almost to the front of the queue, Gareth realised that they had the wrong tickets; they would have to pay extra to take the lift to the top. In order to pay, he would have to leave his place in the queue and go and find the right booth, and he could not leave Rebecca there as a place-holder, at her age (*could he?* he thought, eyeing his daughter and the strangers around her). There was not time to start queuing all over again; he had to get her back to Lionel's flat at a reasonable hour. He gave up their place, and as they walked back down the length of the queue, Gareth tried to explain to Rebecca what had happened. 'They should have put up signs near the *start* of the queue,' he said, before seeing that they had in fact put up plenty of signs. On the stairs that took them back down to ground level, Rebecca kept asking, 'But why, why can't we go to the top?' and in the end, Gareth had been reduced to saying, 'Because we can't.' By the time they reached the metro, she had fallen silent. As they travelled through the tunnels, Gareth closed his eyes and could have slept. When he heard Rebecca telling him, 'This is where we get off,' he was sorry to have to open them again; he had no desire to leave the underground, to return to daylight and Lionel's flat.

He had been walking for a while now without paying attention to his route. Looking around, he realised that he had no idea where he was, other than that he was outside a bar. He went inside. He sat down at the bar and drank a beer, and during his second one he told the barman about Lionel. 'You'd think she was *his* daughter. And the way he laughs–' Mostly the barman listened without speaking, but he seemed to understand. There were other customers as well, visible here and there in the dimly lit room; the barman came and went, and Gareth felt himself relaxing. He ought to stop at two, he thought, and get back to the flat, but he found himself ordering a third, which arrived with a shot. 'I wanted to take her to the catacombs,' said Gareth, 'but they're closed.' He downed the shot. It was getting gloomy outside and Gareth wondered if it would rain and then he realised that it was just late; he had lost track of time. But he saw no harm in staying in the tranquillity of the bar for a while longer.

'Yes,' said the barman. 'But you can still go down, if you want to go alone. You are in the right place.' The barman lifted a hatch in the bar and beckoned to Gareth, who got down off his stool, carefully, as if testing the ground's stability. Behind the bar, the barman was lifting up another hatch, in the floor. He led Gareth down through the opening, down a flight of rickety wooden steps, into a cramped cellar. It smelt of stone and dust and alcohol. The barman was over by the far wall, shifting stacked cases of wine, behind which – Gareth could now see – the cellar extended, although it was bare and unlit back there, and seemed to narrow, like the neck of a bottle. The barman gestured for Gareth to go on through the hole he had made. Gareth stepped into this previously hidden part of the cellar, whose narrowing made it more like a passageway really, or a tunnel. He had a years-old memory of being in an extensive wine cellar whose cool, dim corridor of exquisite and collectable bottles went on and on. He tried to recall where it was, that wine cellar, and then realised that he was only remembering a dream in which, as he walked on, the rows of dark bottles to either side of him became rows of gravestones, as old and cold to the touch as the bottles.

The passageway seemed to be sloping downwards, the way the Dartford Tunnel sloped to take him under the Thames every time he made the trip to Paris, and every time he drove back north. Gareth was still talking to the barman – 'the smell of his cigarette smoke in the bedroom' – when he realised that he was on his own; the barman had other customers upstairs, of course. Later, he would thank him for giving him access to what he assumed was the network of underground tunnels that he had heard of – the ancient mines, of which the catacombs were only a small part. These tunnels had started caving in a couple of hundred years ago, and Gareth did not know how far they extended. Nor was he sure quite where within the network the catacombs were, but he felt sure that he was bound, at any moment, to come face to face with a wall of skulls, a wall of bones. He thought of how he would like to go back and say to Rebecca, in front of Lionel, that he had found a secret passageway into the catacombs, except he did not really want to go back there at all.

In darkness now, he inched his hands along the crumbly walls, feeling his way forward through the cold tunnels. He said aloud, 'I will take you there,' and heard the words echo. The roof of the ever-narrowing tunnel scraped against his scalp and he had to stoop. He could not tell whether he was still heading down or starting to go up. Where the tunnel appeared to fork, he took what seemed, from his blind exploration, the easier way, although he soon found that it sloped sharply downwards. When it forked again, he wondered whether he would be able to find his way back if he wanted to. In that airless corridor, there was no promise of light. He could not even see his own hands. He ought to turn back.

Painting the Walls White

by Michael Stewart

When Will Brotherton was sacked from his factory job he saw it as a door opening. His wife, Kate, however, was angry. What was he going to do now? He explained that he'd always wanted to work for himself. He'd long dreamed about becoming a self-employed painter and decorator. Kate was sceptical, but the next day he went down to Northway Vans and bought a cheap Berlingo. He put an advert in the community magazine and stuck a card in the post office window. He went to the pub and asked around. Nothing.

Two weeks went by before the phone rang. An old woman wanted her window frames painting before the weather turned. He went to the address she had given him and he counted the windows.

'How much?' the old woman asked.

He had some idea of the cost of paint, having decorated his daughter's bedroom a few months ago. The window frames would need sanding and priming first, then undercoating, with two coats of gloss to finish. He gave the woman a price.

The job took nearly three days. The weather was dry and the sky wasn't too cloudy. It was good to work outside with the sun on his skin. He listened to his portable radio and hummed along to the music. There was something very satisfying about painting over the drab paint with a shiny new coat. He was taking something old and rejuvenating it. It felt like a kind of rebirth.

The old woman was happy with the job and paid him in cash. He went to the pub and bought a pint. He sat outside and watched the wind rustle the leaves. This was the life. He was his own boss. He could do what he liked now.

The old woman had told her friends and within a few weeks he was booked up solid. He stopped arguing with Kate. She accepted his new business and was even proud of him. For the first time in months they made love. The work kept coming in and he had to turn people down. He thought about taking someone else on.

But then, as winter came and Christmas approached, the work dried up. No-one wanted the decorators in at Christmas. He was sure it would pick up again in the New Year.

January, though, was as dead as December. He still had a bit of cash left over and he liked spending more time with his daughter. He took her to the park, or, if it was raining, to an indoor play centre with a ball pool. It was good to see her run around with the other kids.

When February came, only a few jobs trickled in and he started to fret. What if he'd made a terrible mistake? Would he have to go back to Mr. Barnett with his tail between his legs and beg for his old job back? The thought chilled him. At night, Kate turned away from him in bed.

Will felt immense relief when he got a phone call from the manager of a warehouse company.

The next day he drove out of town to a new industrial estate next to a motorway. The building was huge, easily the biggest unit on the estate. He rang the bell and was ushered into the waiting area. Five minutes later he was shown around by the manager: a neat man of average height, not much older than Will. He led him into the main room which was like an airport hangar. It was completely empty. The man explained that they were going to fill it with stock soon, but wanted to get it painted first. Was he interested?

Will looked around. It was a massive job. It would take him weeks and weeks to paint it; he wouldn't have to worry about money for at least two months.

'Yes, I can do it. What colour?'

'White.'

It was white already and it didn't really look in need of another coat, but Will kept this thought to himself.

'No problem,' he said. 'White's the cheapest colour.'

Will gave the man a price that he'd inflated quite a bit. He'd need a break after painting this, he thought. The man seemed happy and they shook on it. When Will got home that night, Kate was delighted.

'He's got some more warehouses a bit further out, so if I make a good job of this, he said he'd give me those to do as well.'

'That's brilliant,' said Kate. And she gave him a big smile. That night in bed, she let him cup one of her breasts.

The next day he bought the paint and made his way to the warehouse. The secretary gave him his own key. She said they were only there some of the time, so he'd have to let himself in. She showed him where everything was and then left him to it. He brought some sheets in from the van but realised he wouldn't need them. There was nothing to splash. He had bought extra-large rollers with an extension arm so he could reach the tops of the walls from his ladder. He opened a fresh tub of white paint and poured a generous amount into a black tray. He dipped in the roller, squeezed out the excess paint, and began to paint the white walls white.

It was easy at first, but as he worked it became more difficult to decide where he had painted. He thought of a system. He would paint left to right, starting at the bottom and working his way up. But still, after an hour of this, he kept forgetting where he had got to. You had to catch the wet paint with the light on it because it reflected the light better than dry paint. After another hour his eyes started playing tricks on him. The white was straining his eyes and he could no longer tell which was wet and which was dry paint. He came up with another plan. He took out a pencil and marked up a portion of the wall, then he took a section and marked it up into squares. This way he could easily tell where he had got to.

He grafted till past one o'clock, then sat down in a corner on the unused dust sheets and ate his sandwiches. He poured himself coffee from his flask and listened to the radio. He surveyed his progress. He'd been working for over four hours and he had hardly made a dent in it. The wall was vast and he'd only painted about three or four percent. He'd be lucky to have finished ten percent by the end of the day. Ten days to paint that one wall, and then there were three others. Forty days. That was well within his estimate of fifty days. If he kept at it, at the same rate, he'd be able to take a few days off before the next job. Another warehouse the same size as this one. Also painted white.

On the drive home, all he could see were white walls. All he could smell was the tang of white paint.

He was very quiet that night when he and Kate sat down for their evening meal.

'Are you ok?' she asked.

'Fine.'

He went to bed early and dreamed he was painting a white wall white. When he stepped back, he could not see where the wall started or where it ended. He woke up and stared at the clock. It was 5am. He lay back again but couldn't sleep. All he could think about were white walls. Endless white walls.

That day he worked hard, trying to shake off the dream. He turned up the radio and sang along to the music at the top of his voice. His voice echoed in the empty chamber.

After work, he called into his local pub and had a pint.

'Where have you been?'

He explained that painting walls was thirsty work. Kate didn't seem to mind that much. The next evening he stopped for two pints and she commented again. He apologised, but a pattern soon formed: calling in for a skinful on the way home; arguing with Kate when he got back. At night he'd have the same dream, in which he'd wake up inside a white cube with no way in or out. Then he'd wake up again.

In the warehouse, no matter how loud he played the radio, he found he couldn't concentrate. He tried to sing along to the music but the words would blur and the white walls undulated in front of his eyes. He stared into the tubs of white paint and recalled the bottomless well in a story he'd read as a kid. It had always terrified him. He imagined falling down into the endless whiteness.

That night they argued.

'How many have you had?' she said.

'I don't know, I don't keep count,' he slurred.

'You'll get stopped by the police.'

He shrugged.

'Or worse. You'll end up killing someone. Is that what you want?'

He shrugged again.

'You're drinking away the profits, Will. What's the point in that?'

'I don't give a fuck!'

'You don't give a fuck about us then, do you? You don't give a fuck about your daughter. You don't give a fuck about me.'

He lowered his voice, 'Look, Kate, I don't think I can do it anymore.'

'What do you mean?'

'The job. I don't think I can finish it.'

'Why not? It's easy enough, isn't it? It's good money. You're your own boss. Isn't that what you wanted?'

He was being unreasonable, in her eyes. He'd been sacked from a perfectly good job once more, but had set up his own business. Now he'd made a success of it. He'd secured a big contract, giving him months and months of steady work.

He went to bed early that night. Kate put her hand on his shoulder when she came to bed later, but he pretended to be asleep.

The next day he drove out to the warehouse and gave himself a good talking to. 'Come on, Will, be a man. You can do this. It's not like you're working down a mine or working outside in the middle of winter. It's not the Somme. It's easy work. No heavy lifting. No danger.'

He turned the radio on and opened a tub of fresh paint. He marked off the sections he planned to do that day and got cracking. He was working on the top parts of the wall and had to fully extend the ladder to get into the corners. The ladder started to wobble. He took it easy. The concrete floor was a long way down. He'd smash his bones to pieces if he lost his balance. But as he stared at the white wall, at the old dry white paint and the new wet white paint, he felt himself becoming disorientated. Which way was up and which way was down? The ladder was shaking. He tried to keep as still as possible, but the ladder kept on shaking. He looked down. Yes, that was down. And it was a long way. He would break his back or his neck if he fell. The ground seemed to disappear beneath him. He was falling into the well and there was nothing to hold on to as the white walls rushed past, the whiteness engulfing him.

Eventually the ladder stopped shaking and he slowly climbed back down. He lay on the floor and stared at the white ceiling and the white walls. He was surrounded by white. Imprisoned by it. This was hell. Not fire and brimstone, just a huge cube of whiteness. He couldn't see beyond it. He didn't know how he was ever going to get past it.

'A pint of lager and a whisky chaser.'

It wasn't even three o'clock but he was done for the day. He sat in a corner, necked the whisky in one and gulped down the lager. He went back to the bar and reordered, necking the drinks once more. He tried to get the image of the white walls out of his mind. The vast cube of white all around him. Something was on the telly in the other corner of the pub, but he couldn't make any sense of it. There were a few other people in the pub now. Solo drinkers. Workers clocking off early, or people on benefits. He bought another round.

It was eight o'clock already. He should be going home. Kate would be wondering where he was. She'd be worried about him. He went to the bar and ordered one more for the road. When he tried to pay the barmaid, his change spilled over the floor. Coins rolled under tables and chairs. He stared at them, incapable of picking them up. The room was spinning. He clung to the bar and took out a crumpled ten pound note.

'Are you ok?' the barmaid said as she took the note. He sat back down in the corner with his drinks. There were more people in now. Or was he seeing double? The room was moving. He kept forgetting where he was. Good, that was the idea: he wanted to forget where he was and who he was.

It was gone nine when he came round to the barmaid shaking his arm.

'You can't behave like this in here,' she said. 'You'll have to go home.'

She was staring down on him with a look of horror. He looked back at her uncomprehending.

'You've had enough,' she said. 'You're disturbing the other customers.'

A pint glass was smashed on the table in front.

'Don't come back. You're barred.'

He woke up at the bottom of the stairs, fully dressed. His head was banging. He stumbled to his feet. Outside his van was parked at an angle to the road. There was a dint in one of the panels. His wife had left a note: *we need to talk*.

After a cold shower, he set off for work but found himself pulling into a different pub. All day he sat there drinking. Other drinkers were chatting at the bar. A couple close by were holding hands. He stared at the glass in front and raised it to his lips. He remembered when Kate had first held his hand. They had met in a pub. She was friends with someone from work who introduced them. They said hello but they were both a bit shy. He'd got her number and they'd arranged to meet in a bar a few days later. Conversation had been awkward at first, but they found they had a lot in common and soon she was smiling and laughing at his jokes. It was towards the end of the night. He was walking out with her and it had just happened. Her hand in his, like a miracle.

Outside, the cold night air sobered him up a little. It was snowing, and must have been snowing for hours. Where had he parked the van? All the vehicles were covered. He meandered across the carpark, tripped and fell. He lay back in the snow and was surrounded by whiteness. He stared at the sky, now filled with tumbling snowflakes, and felt them land on his body and face.

Thick cold white blobs. He couldn't see out of his eyes. He could feel his blood cooling and his heart slowing …

Busy at the bar now … Hardly move … Where had his beer gone? … There was Kate, holding his hand, as she had on their first date. Her hand was warm and smooth. But the night wasn't over. She was enjoying herself too much to go home. Did he know a bar they could go to for one final drink? He knew just the place, where they could get one last beer and whisky chaser. One for the road.

Prohibition

by Cathy Galvin

Tom watched the girl descending into the valley. She seemed to float in the lilac light of the mountains, not far from where he dragged the lily flowers from the lake, his spade slicing beneath their bulbs. He watched as the light faded and the eldest daughter of Michael Flaherty was finally close. She wore a shawl, her black hair cut short, walking the cow towards him.

He greeted her, led her to his house. She had come barefoot, miles through the bog, with no-one to guide her. Tom's wife Mary blessed her at the door, tearful at the thought of the journey the girl had made to provide milk for her small children.

Michael Flaherty had been true to his word. His daughter Anne had walked from dawn until dusk. Mary washed and warmed the girl's feet, poured thin potato broth into a bowl. The girl drank, holding the bowl like a chalice.

Tom saw that Anne was nervous, eager to please. He saw how she would look at you, look at a man, sideways. She held the shawl close, trying to hide herself, but he could see the stains of mud on her white leg, darkening above her knee. He looked away. How old might she be: fifteen?

Mary settled Anne near the hearth on the earth floor. A black pot bubbled over the fire, simmering the musky lily bulbs from the lake. She would use their purple dye in her weaving. She told Anne what a good girl she was, to come so far to help her family after they had to sell their cow.

Tom pulled at the leather strap on a hook by the window of his bedroom, running his razor along its length. When it was sharpened, he poured warm water from a kettle into a bowl, found his soap and brush and began to shave by candlelight. His face puddled in the stained mirror, indistinct, but he could see well enough to scrape the grey stubble from his face and neck.

He left the door ajar so that he could listen to the women in the adjoining room, and heard how the girl had been afraid on her journey. His wife was whispery, soothing.

Can I, Anne was saying, *Can I tell you a secret, Mary?*

Of course you can, my lamb.

Please promise, the girl said, *please promise you will not tell my mother. She mustn't know.*

She told Mary everything.

Tom thought of other voices: of women he'd walked beside over twenty years before, when he and Anne's father had crossed the Atlantic from Ireland to America. They would walk towards the Broadway Theatre in Boston listening to the murmur of women flowing past in pretty shoes, their skirts clinging, his body burning. Up for the dancing, ices, and singing. Urging him and Michael to visit them in the hotels where they worked as maids and waitresses in Maine. *What fine voices you have, Michael and Tom. Shan't we be gay? It's so lonesome without you. When shall we see you again?* One woman sent him a letter on embossed paper: *It's my pleasure to write to you since I know you would not write to me.* He kept it, took it out of its envelope occasionally, touched it. The handwriting looped. It was too fine for him to respond in his own clumsy, unschooled hand.

Tom and Michael had travelled from Connemara on the White Star Line in 1921, to work for The New York, New Haven and Hartford Railway Company, cleaning the train carriages late at night, telling everyone they met they were engineers. They booked passage on ships for their brothers and cousins to join them, sending money when they could.

Michael, Tom had always thought, paid a high price for

high ideals: his evening classes in technical drawing; three dollars a month to the Foresters of America as an insurance against funeral fees and sickness; his upscale boarding house; and hundreds of dollars to the campaign for Irish Freedom. Paying for a new suit, bow-tie and white shirt, to have his photo taken at the Walper Studio on Washington Street, to send home. Paying with the certainty of a man who believed in progress. One of Michael's favourite songs was 'The Victory Loan' and Tom knew he believed every word of every verse:

Then up the Republic of Erin,
And long live the President too;
We will rally around De Valera
Be his enemies many or few.
We bring not the sword of a soldier
Nor rifle nor cannon alone,
But a weapon of power for each holder,
A bond for her Victory Loan.

Tom, by contrast, believed in very little. There would be a great life for them in America, Michael had persuaded him, despite the stories of young people taking their own lives rather than return to Ireland penniless. For a while, there was enough work. When the jobs and money began to run out it felt inevitable to Tom. They belonged not in the city, but in the overworked stony fields and on the unforgiving sea.

Michael appeared unaware of defeat, of any humiliation in the thought of returning home, switching his allegiance from America to the promises of the Irish Free State so seamlessly, so eloquently: *Tom, it is our right to secure our happiness and independence in our own land. It is our right to speak our own words in Irish and make ours a land to be proud of. No more silence. No more begging. No more old men lamenting on the roads of Connemara. No more women holding the cold bodies of their babies. No more indignity for man. No more thirsting.*

At least, that was how Tom remembered Michael's words. He recalled feeling only an empty sickness as he listened. Hopes never fulfilled. Thoughts of the dead, hanging in their twelve-dollar rooms in Boston, never spoken of, and of those unseen descendants, buried in unmarked graves along the roadsides at home, forgotten. Endless talk of the end of imperialism, of ideals and nation. Great men and women urging everyone to speak the Gaelic language he and Michael had spoken from birth, but which marked them out as uneducated and poor.

There was a clearer memory: a bitter evening in southern Boston, slanting rain turning snow into sludge. The Green Lamp Tea Room was still open: couples seated near the window; four men at one table, five at another further behind.

The girl with short black hair sat alone. Tom told himself she had been waiting for him. He asked to sit at her table, ordered a pot of tea for two from a waiter whose eyes did not meet his.

Tom poured cold opaque liquid into china tea-cups; sipped and felt the white spirit catch his throat, burning into his bones and belly. The tannin lining of the pot gave an earthiness to the sharp gin. Or was it poteen? Despite the ban on the sale of liquor, he knew all the places where it could be bought: the cafés; the garages; the places where women would slip you a bottle from inside their coat or from their baby carriage. The waiter had left them a bowl of sugar and jug of milk. The girl carefully poured the milk into her cup, stirred sugar into her cold cocktail. Looked at him. Grey eyes. Hiding. Scared.

He poured himself another drink, noticed the shake in his hands as he placed his cup on the saucer. What would be the point of words? They knew why they were here. He would not tell her she was beautiful as a lily. He would not tell her this was the last night he would spend in the city. He would not tell her there was nothing to believe in. She had bitten nails. White hands. Tiny, blue-veined wrists.

She told him she was hungry, thirsty. He bought her slices of sponge cake, a full jug of milk and, for himself, a second pot of the special tea. He drank it quickly. The waiter closed the curtains across the windows and Tom thought of home: of the barn where his mother slept at night to keep away from his father. Its smell. The thumping and grunting he had heard coming from the barn one night as he had stepped outside to look at the stars. He finished the tea quickly. Later, in his room, he drank from a bottle. The girl lifted her skirts, like petals, and turned her face away.

Pressing into her, he felt her limpness, smelled milk, blood, unwashed linen. Her passivity was another death. His anger, at her, himself, the futility of some search for grace, also flared and died. When she dressed to leave, he handed her five dollars, saw her coat was short in the arms, her bruised wrists hanging. He spoke: *Nice coat.* She told him it was the coat she had been given when she left Ireland, aged thirteen, two years before. *I'll be buried in it.* She let the money fall.

In the years following their return home, Michael had embellished his decision to leave, even to Tom, boasting of the house and land he had bought near the shore from the widow Walsh; never mentioning that the money had come from the dowry he was given on marriage to his second cousin Kate. *What was there for us in America?* he had said to Tom. *Laughing and dancing and sending money home. Saving every penny for the fine clothes and not able to eat a decent meal. Wondering where the next job would come from, and always the talking and the chatter and the blather and no pride or grace in that.*

In August 1934, Michael showed Tom a letter he had received from Roinn An Uachtarain, the Department of the President in Dublin, signed by Eamon de Valera, President of the Executive Council of the Irish Free State:

> On behalf of the Irish people I take this opportunity to thank the American citizens who subscribed to the External Loans of the Irish Republic. They trusted and helped us in our time of need. It is a privilege to return the money that they lent us. The debt of gratitude we owe them is, however, one that we can never fully repay.

Michael appeared agitated, excited: *We made our future with the men and women who spilled blood on the steps of the Post Office in Dublin. Who stood shoulder to shoulder and sacrificed themselves for us. So that we could speak in our own tongue, sing to God as free men, live on the land of our ancestors, the land that is ours by every right of natural justice and of blood.*

Tom did not say to Michael they were both getting old, with bills they could not pay and children they could not feed. Did not say, the return of the loan would not stop Michael's children from having to leave home to find work in England before they were fully grown. Did not ask, what exactly had Michael spent his money on: a new puritanism, a false pride?

Tom saw his fields, year by year, yielding meagre crops. To feed his family, he had sold first a horse, then a donkey, then one cow, then another. Shame looked out at him from the eyes of his children.

He often watched Michael in church at Sunday Mass. Shoulders back. Always a pew or two ahead. Michael was a man you could confess things to. He was a man who could persuade you to cross an ocean to another world, then persuade you to return to a worse one. A man, when you feared your children were starving, who would send his cow to you with his daughter. Tom knew there was little in Michael's house. A scrap of a son he worked hard out in the bog. Another girl, who had left to work in the hospital in Galway. A wife with a sunken face, hair pulled back, her breasts flattened sacks. Everything tight against her bones. And there was Anne.

As Tom shaved by candlelight, he listened carefully to his wife and Michael Flaherty's daughter. Anne told her the story of why she had been afraid, walking alone to their cottage with the cow. Of the man who followed her in the fields at home; of how she had learned to run away if she caught sight of him.

The first time he had approached her, she said, his face had been hidden in a dark scarf up to his eyes, cap pulled down. As he drew near, she noticed his hands moving inside his jacket. *Do you want to see the little flower?* His hands were holding something fleshy and she had run.

Another time, he was behind her before she had time to see or hear him, one hand inside her clothes, the other bruising her shoulder as he pressed her against the rock of the field wall. He had touched her *there*, she said, *below*.

He scratched me, Mary, she said, *He scratched me there till I bled.* She had broken away, run, not turned back. Her mother must not know, it would break her heart. Her mother had argued with their father, telling him girls should not be working in the fields or crossing the valleys without a chaperone. *What is there that could harm them, woman?* he had replied.

Tom could not forget Michael's vanity in Boston: his

curled, oiled hair. Those airs; pride in his well-cut clothes and the way he carried himself, shoulders back. Always reading a book. Michael, believing in the dignity of the life De Valera preached. His children in rags. His wife sunken. His daughter sent out through the bog, alone, to any man who crossed her path. To him. Tom.

He thought of the girl in Boston with the short black hair. He had not known how or when to stop. Had told her to be quiet. Put his hand over her mouth, though he thought he could still hear her. He felt he was sinking into blue night, into a black lake, digging deep for the roots – of what? Not her. Not himself. They were both delicate and damned, in a place where they did not belong and had nothing to believe in. She had bled. His hands pushed her down into the mattress, the brittle feel of her breaking open a flood that rose from his feet to his belly, that pushed her further down as he knelt on her shoulders, pouring over her mouth. After, he gave her a glass of moonshine. She spat into a basin.

Michael was a fool. Offering his cow to a man when his own family needed milk. Sending his daughter across the bog and mountain. Alone. Afraid. Hungry. Thirsty.

Tom knew that he would wake early. He had seen the curve of Anne's waist in her cotton shift, the puckering of small nipples against cold cloth. Tomorrow, he would walk into the field beyond the house. He would watch and wait, resting his weight on a spade until Anne emerged, pulling the shawl around herself as she said goodbye to Mary and began the long walk home. He would make no noise as he followed her into the palm of the valley. He would take his time, draw near enough to smell her warmth, to see the nape of her neck below short black hair.

He felt his face. Stubble gone. Clean.

He felt for the bottle inside his jacket.

Just One More

by Jonathan Taylor

Mate, you know you want to. One more isn't going to hurt, is it?

Fuck the doctor. And Janey. Just for tonight. It's a special occasion. Even Janey can see that, surely. It's hardly every night Noel's off to get hitched, is it?

Okay, mate, I know he used to live his whole life like it's a fucking stag-do. Course. But this is his *actual real* stag-do. So switch off that fucking phone and enjoy yourself for once. Come on, get that down you. Just one more.

I'm telling you, sod the doctor. What does she know? What harm is one night going to do? And you never know what'll happen on a night like tonight. Anything's possible with you, me, Noel and Gabriel all out together. Like old uni nights. Good times.

Rare occasion these days, all us out together. Tonight's like a reunion – see it that way. Six years on. Back to the good times, before we all got bogged down with life and women and shit. Wish those days'd come back. And to-night, mate, tonight perhaps they can. So don't waste it. Make the most of it, for fuck's sake. Tonight's the night.

I mean, look at those *chavettes* over there. All shapes and sizes. Slim, fat, ugly. From up the estate probably. Common as muck, thick as pig shit. Not a GCSE to rub between them. And you can tell they're on the pull, the way they're trussed up. Short skirts, high heels, tits out. God, look at the tits on that one – don't even know why she's bothering with a top. Have anyone, that sort – you know it, I know it. We'll get them over. Have a bit of fun with them. Flash them our wallets. Sweet talk them with our jobs and cars and shit. They'll be wet before you can say *Audi Cabriolet*.

Fuck's sake. You scared them off. Miserable bastard. You didn't need to tell them about Janey and your Chloë straight away, did you? Makes us all look bad. Bloody hell, mate, don't ruin it for Noel. He needs one last blow out. Pull yourself together, for fucking Noel's sake, for…

Okay, okay, I'm sorry, mate. Have this on me. Yeah, I know, it sucks. I do get it. I do understand it's been, like, tough for you, since…

Yeah, I know, it's shit, you've told me about it. So many times. No guy needs a wife who won't put out. I can see she's, like, *still* upset and not in the mood. I can see Janey's the sort who mightn't cope with stuff. She always was highly strung. High maintenance, that one. I know that from when *we* were an item. Still, it's been – what? – nearly two years, since …

Well, okay, eighteen months, whatever. But all that time not to … I mean, fuck's sake, what's the point of getting married if you can't get it on a plate?

Fair enough, I can see why she's still so pissed off, and you've had to use kid gloves on her. I mean, with what happened to your girl two years ago … okay, whatever, eighteen months. Fucking hell. What could be worse than losing a daughter like that? You know how we all felt for you, mate, at the funeral. Fucking awful. Poor girl. Poor Chloë. No-one deserves that. She was robbed – whole life in front of her. You can be sure if we – y'know, me, Noel, Gabriel – ever found the bastard who was driving that van, *we'd* run *him* over. And then fucking reverse. What are mates for? God, what a bastard, scarpering like that, leaving her in the road. World's full of bastards.

But we're eighteen months or two years or whatever down the line now, and you and Janey, well, you're still here, aren't you? Gotta get out. Drink and forget. Know what I mean? We've all listened over and over again, you know that. Fair enough – it's the sort of thing mates do for each other. And you had to get it off your chest. But tonight's not the night, is it? It's not like Chloë would've wanted you to go on like this, would she? She was a go-getting kinda girl, from what I saw. An angel, like, who was always smiling, even when … well, you know when. Fuck's sake, she was smiling when they shut the lid.

Okay, less of that. Do me a favour. Leave that wet shit for Janey and the mother-in-law. Remember it's Noel's night tonight. Not yours. Look, have another and you'll feel better. Like medicine. Just one more. Here you go.

*

Look at it this way, mate. Tonight, it's like a holiday from girlfriends and wives and exes and all that everyday shit. God, I need a holiday from the Ex like you wouldn't believe. Tonight's like an island, a fucking island from everything else. Nothing before, nothing after. What happens on a stag stays on a stag, as they say.

Most important, we need to make sure Noel has a good time. So have another and think about this. Just an idea. Those slags we saw earlier, they're still around somewhere in here. In fact, look, there they are – by the bar – over there. Over *there*, you blind fuck. Anyway, I've been talking to Gabriel and Noel, and I reckon – no, we *all* reckon – we should have another go at them. I mean, look at the state of them. They blew us out before, but they're even more shit-faced now. Desperate for cock. They'll never resist a charm offensive from us. You know you want to. I mean, your Janey mightn't feel like putting out, but you're a bloke, and blokes are different. Blokes have to, or their balls burst.

Look, I tell you what, the place is going to shut in a bit. We'll follow them out.

All we need is one of them.

*

Don't sweat it. It's all taken care of. Have another – just one to, like, steady your nerves. Just one more.

Honest, it's all sorted. Gabriel's nipped out to get his car ready. He's not shit-faced like you or me, so he'll be okay. He's going to pull up near the club. Black Audi, black windows, no-one's going to see anything.

Then all we need, like I said, is *one* of them – get her away from her friends. Distract them with some shit, and nab her. Shove her in the Audi – then … well, then we'll all have a bit of fun, her included.

Just one more, Dutch courage and all that shit, mate.

Oh come on, we owe it to Noel. *You* owe it to him for scaring the slags off before. And we owe it to ourselves – I mean, life's been so shitty since uni. Work, bills, divorce. I tell you, I spend every daylight hour at the moment talking to solicitors, or being screamed at down the phone by Mrs. Bitch-Ex. Fuck's sake: it's her who had the affair, her who banged some doped-up social worker behind my back – yet it's me who gets all the shit. Me who has to pay, apparently. So you see, mate, it's not like it's been fucking Christmas for me either, these last few years. I know you've had to put with a tonne of crap – but so have we all. And now's a chance to have a laugh for a change. So don't mess it up for everyone, mate.

Look, have this last shot – it'll sort you out. Just one more and then we're on. We're on, mate. Gabriel's just text me to say it's ready. He's revving the car as we speak. Probably revving something else, too, knowing Gabriel.

Oh shut up, mate, enough with the worrying. Janey's never going to know, nor is Mrs. Bitch-Ex, nor are all the bastard solicitors circling me. God, *she* can shag anyone she likes, apparently, but I'm meant to be whiter than white. Well, fuck that tonight. None of them's ever gonna know.

The girl herself probably won't know, she'll be so pissed. And if she does remember tomorrow, well, the pigs, they're realistic. Even if she does report us, they know just how much effort to put into a case like this. They're filthy up on the estate. You know it, the pigs know it. They do this sort of thing all the time. Back of the car gangbang, four good-looking lads – four loaded execs. Patent leather seats. She'll be fucking honoured.

Mate, what're you going on about? What's this got to do with your Chloë? Perhaps the doctor's right after all. You're not right up there, mate. This slut isn't your Chloë. Different fucking class. The one we get, she's no-one's daughter – least not for tonight. Probably never was, if you know what I mean: most of them don't have dads up on the estate. Or they have loads of dads. Single mums, the lot of them.

Honestly, mate, shut up about your Chloë. This hasn't got anything to do with her. Think of Noel. Think of fucking *loyalty*. It's all us lads've got – loyalty to each other. We have to stick together, because, believe me, your wife, Noel's fiancée, all of them are at it behind our backs. You think Janey's not, or wouldn't if she got the chance? Wake up, mate. Look what happened to me, what Mrs. Bitch-Ex did to me.

Where d'you think you're going?

Fuck you, then. Yeah, fuck you. And your dead daughter. And Janey. Fuck you all. Go back to them, if that's what you want, to be shafted behind your back. Some mate you turned out to be.

Our Lady of Penrhys
by Desmond Barry

We're all listening to nineties Black Metal. Burzum, Euronymous and Blackthorn. Norwegian stuff. And we're sitting in the front room of Palsy's house and it's all getting a bit mad. Palsy's got this big bottle a speed. He's done a chemists down in Ponty and come out with this big sweetie jar full. Any time anyone feels like they're coming down a bit they just reach into the jar on the coffee table and swallow a few more and wash them down with a slug from a bottle a Strongbow.

It's getting a bit freaky I have to say. I gave up speed ages ago. I gone all natural like. Seasonal you might say. Right now, it's mushroom time and they're growing all over the mountain. I collected about three hundred the other day and I got them in a big plastic bag that I put on the table next to the sweetie jar. None a the others can be bothered with the mushies though. They're off their tits on the speed and they're pouring down the Strongbow … and Blackthorn, funnily enough … and Festival Vat.

Thing is with mushies, it could go either way, but for some reason, I just feel blissed out and loved up even though Emma's got the corpse paint out and she's slathering Billy Deadman from his forehead to his undies with this thick white mess and splashing it with red to make it look all bloody and rotten, like he's a zombie. Which he is in a way.

Out the window, there's a procession going by. All these Catholics out on a pilgrimage. They're walking through the housing estate, up the hill toward the mountain path, where there's this old Christian shrine and a big statue of a woman with a crown holding a kid and standing on top of a pillar: Our Lady of Penrhys, that is. Been there for centuries, it has. Well, had. It's all a bit of a reconstruction like … close by the well that's supposed to have healing powers.

It might like. You never know. Good for the eyes and the rheumatic.

Pen Rhys means Rhys's head. Supposedly old Rhys, a Welsh king or something, had it cut off by the English back in the day. Like these nutters in Syria now. No wonder it's so fucking violent up here. Build a village on a site like that, innit?

But it's the well they come for. Out on the mountain the Virgin Mary appeared in an oak tree to a few shepherds back in the Middle Ages. And where she appeared, there she left a wooden statue, and nobody could get the statue out of the tree until they'd built a shrine and a chapel. Like divine blackmail. I suppose. So they did. And then Henry VIII burned the shrine and chapel down and burned the statue in London. Just like the Middle East today, innit?

All of which reminds me of Varg Vikernes — the Black Metal Nazi — burning down that church in Norway. He's Billy Deadman's hero. How you can have Varg Vikernes as a hero is beyond me. He's a Class-A nutter who stabbed Euronymous to death. Came out on parole a couple of years ago after serving time for about nine years. I can't imagine he's changed that much. But you never know.

Billy Deadman is dead against all the Penrhys Catholics. He wanted to burn down the church in the centre of Tylorstown but his girlfriend Emma put him off.

Satanists and Nazis, Henry VIII and the Taliban. I mean, for fuck's sake. Can we all get along here? Thing is. Here I am in a room full of wannabe black metal freaks all out of their heads on Palsy's speed or all pissed up on Strongbow. They been out a their heads for about three days. And it's getting a bit freaky.

Palsy puts Blackthorn on the sound system and it's like he's opened the gates of Hell.

Blackthorn? Named after the cider or what? That'll open the gates of Hell for you.

So here's Billy Deadman. He pulls a big fucking serrated knife out of his rucksack that he'd hidden under the coffee table and he holds his arms open in the form of a cross. Emma stands in front of him and paints a slash of red across his mouth like Heath Ledger as the Joker. For some reason the mushies are keeping me incredibly mellow — never mind the guitar screech and the growl of the vocals — or Deadman, stripped to the waist covered in corpse paint, who is now thrashing away on the air guitar with a twelve-inch serrated knife as a plectrum.

Emma starts a jerky dance, her blonde hair flailing all around her.

I can hear a faint vocal from the hymn-singing procession.

Mary most pure, star of the sea...

Then it's drowned out as Palsy cranks up the volume.

Deadman looks out the window.

Listen, he shouts over the thrash. They all come up here singing their fucking hymns and saying their rosaries ... Kiddy-fiddling priests and faggy altar boys waving around their fucking incense burners and all them old ladies in their perms and raincoats ... fucking hell ... we gotta do something ... this is our place not theirs.

I can't help thinking it's gonna be like fucking *Game of Thrones* up here in a minute.

I need to chill. I spark up a ciggy. Step past the bouncing knees. The banging heads. The pumping fists. And I'm out in the tiny hallway where I can open the door and get some fresh air.

And for the first time, the grunt and grind of the metal

coming through the wall makes me think something awful is going to happen.

The weirdness of it. The procession is going up the mountain path to the shrine and the statue. A few of the smarter people on the estate have got their stalls out. They're selling rosaries and little medallions with a picture of the statue on them.

All those sincere voices singing that hymn:

Pray-ay for the wanderer, pray for me...

I duck away as Deadman, bollock naked like a Viking berserker erupts from the house, waving his twelve-inch serrated knife and speaking in Satanic tongues.

Oh shit!

Arrga garba groffin yaga gurber zambo yaaargh!

Fair play to Deadman ... I can see his point ... the awful hypocrisy of the kiddy-fiddling cover-up ... the priest out in front there with a bald bloke in a black cassock and white surplice behind him carrying a cross on a long pole that waves around in the dry air of the freak heat wave and an odd white cloud drifts above the round mountain top with the dry pines below and the ferns turning brown and I think how desperate they are to believe in something... how desperate we all are... from the growl of the vocals in the house behind me and the thrash of the guitar discordant dis-harmonic demonic ... And the naked Deadman waving the knife ... and Emma screams: for fuck's sake, Billy, get back inside!

Whether it's a miracle or not — brought on by Emma or the Virgin Mary – the rage drains out of him and he goes back in the house.

Come on, love, Emma says, let's go upstairs.

And the mushies keep me warm inside, and I step away from the doorstep and glide down the concrete path where the terrified tail end of the procession passes by the market stalls with their icons and holy imagery and I hope they haven't called the cops … and on they go like medieval penitents praying for the end of the world and the opening of the gates of heaven to see them out of this loveless and desolate world where all they hold dear turns to obscenity and horror dressed up in the red of cardinals' robes, the bloated and the deadly, the skull and the maggot, the graves of orphaned children abandoned to the sisters of mercilessness, the bastards in the dole office who cut off your benefits, the bastards in parliament who get disabled people evicted because of the bedroom tax … and Deadman yelling Satanic curses … and still they sing, I can hear them on the mountainside…

Mary most pure, star of the sea…

And behind me the growl of Burzum…

All of us staring into a fucking bleak nothingness … the blue of the sky … Cloud shadows drifting across the green mountain top … and that statue … the woman with the crown and the kid in her arms … centuries of hope for love and wisdom … all there in the statue of the mammy and the babby. If only … I mean … if only…

Back in the house Emma and Deadman have gone upstairs … they're in bed … I imagine the serrated twelve-inch knife is on the floor beside them … Emma curled up in Billy Deadman's arms … willing him on … to keep banging her despite the speed that every passing moment threatens to shrivel his dick …

And me? I squat and watch the sunset as the pilgrims drift away … back down the valley … and brown smoke rises against the deep blue twilit sky … where off in the distance a kiddy has lit a match … and the flames catch … and the dry ferns crackle to light up the horizon in a line of orange fire.

Calling Time

by Sue Wilsea

1981

Trouble's brewing in south London. You can smell it in the air. People have been flocking into the Law Centre all day, many restless. Jill tries to shut out the background noise and focus on a particularly tricky asylum claim but snippets of conversation keep floating into her consciousness.

It's police brutality, man ...

Stop and search, no way is that gonna keep happening...

At least we're ready this time ...

At lunchtime she walks round the block in an unsuccessful attempt to shift a pounding headache. Huddles of youths are on street corners and she's overcome with an urge to leave work early and collect Ally and Jasmine from school. Returning to the office, she makes her excuses to her line manager who's sympathetic: Jill's a highly effective member of the team who has rarely taken time off in the four years she's worked there. How she manages to do an Open University degree and bring up two daughters by herself he can't imagine.

That night the world explodes. Police sirens; shouting and screaming; thuds as police batons hit riot shields; feet pounding on pavements; flames crackling. Jill keeps the curtains shut and distracts the girls by playing Cabbage Patch dolls. She's no idea whether they're safe here but she's decided this is where they'll stay. She has every sympathy with civil unrest: the previous year she was in Bristol after the St. Paul's riots to give free legal advice to young black men. She's marched and demonstrated, signed petitions and lobbied Parliament, but now her priority has to be for her two darling girls who are in the kitchen giggling and making popcorn. At each pop Jill flinches.

Outside, a splintering sound as car windows are broken. Her hands tremble. In a cupboard under the book shelves there's a bottle of vodka. Jill hasn't had a drink since the night she almost lost everything: she keeps the vodka here as proof to herself that she can resist. She's opened the cupboard door before, even lifted the bottle out, unscrewed the cap and inhaled its fumes, but has never yet had a drink.

Now a squabble between the girls starts in the kitchen and outside it sounds as if people are jumping on a car roof. Jill claps her hands over her ears.

1968

Clare and Jill first meet in the High Street Wimpy Bar. Clare should have been meeting her best friend but she hasn't turned up. There are no free seats, so it's dead embarrassing hovering near the door and trying not to check her watch too often. Suddenly, her eyes meet those of a girl who's sitting with a big group by the window. This girl, who Clare later discovers to be Jill, elbows the boy sitting next to her and pats the free bit of red banquette. Clare squeezes in and says thanks. Jill is chewing bubble gum and nods at Clare before turning her back. The group are noisy: two boys are messing about with tomato-shaped sauce containers, holding them like guns and pretending to fire at one another. They are getting looks from other customers. A waitress tells them that they all need to order something or they can 'sling their hook.'

'Fascist,' mutters Jill, popping a bubble, 'All right, I'll have a Coke then.'

The others order and the waitress looks at Clare, tapping her pencil on her pad.

She panics, 'I'll have a Coke too.'

Clare is not allowed Coke. Or bubble gum. Instantly she worries that her mother will abandon her usual Saturday morning routine, come into town and discover her in the Wimpy Bar (also not allowed). Jill has straightened hair and wears so much eye make-up that her eyelids look weighted down. Her mini skirt is what Clare's mother would call a pelmet. She's wearing white plastic boots and her chipped nail polish matches her purple skinny rib. Clare thinks she looks fab and can't wait to draw her.

Although at school Jill's in a different stream to Clare, they start hanging out together. This has earned disapproval from the girls in Clare's form who call Jill 'rough' and 'easy,' but Clare likes the way her new friend doesn't give a toss about anything: she makes the V sign to teachers behind their backs and regularly gets detentions. They spend dinnertimes in the Art Room where Jill, usually fidgety and restless, agrees to sit for Clare. While Clare struggles to capture those high cheekbones and coffee-coloured skin, Jill talks about boys and Clare tries not to be shocked. Lots of boys ask Jill out but she only accepts those who have money and their own wheels. She lost her virginity to an uncle last Christmas, aged thirteen, so sex is no big deal. If she's taken out somewhere nice, treated like a lady and given lots of wine then she will let men fuck her.

At the fourth year Christmas disco Jill introduces Clare to vodka and lime. Squashed together in a smelly toilet cubicle, they swig the sweet sticky drink. Although her head is buzzing, Clare enjoys the music much more than usual when they return to dancing. Later, at her front door, she throws up onto the rose bed but manages to convince her mother the culprit is a dodgy sausage roll. In time, she can keep at least five vodkas down. She discovers that lime also goes well with lager; that snowballs are sweet and frothy;

that the Dubonnet and lemonade her parents occasionally let her have is more sophisticated than the Black Velvet Jill downs in pints.

1972

Clare is at Leeds University studying Art History. She wanted to go to Art School but her mother said she wasn't good enough. She lives in Hall and for the first time meets Northerners who eat strange things, like chip butties, and say what they think.

Jill visits during her first term. She had difficulty thumbing lifts and arrives bad-tempered and hungry. Clare hasn't managed to buy food. Her first long essay is due and she's frightened of her tutor. She makes Jill toast before going to the Student Union, where they both get drunk very quickly. It's not the buzzy, floaty drunkenness of their younger years, but a dark oppressive feeling which makes each resentful of the other. Clare tries introducing Jill to her new friends, but there's mutual distrust. Jill makes it clear she thinks the University lot are snobbish and self-important; for their part, once they've discovered she works in a shoe shop, they think it's really funny to keep requesting 'These Boots are Made for Walking' and 'Blue Suede Shoes'.

Later they go to a disco in a nearby boys' hall. Jill's wearing a white lace mini dress and under the strobe lighting her underwear is visible. She attracts a lot of attention and, fuelled by more shots, her dancing gets increasingly wild. When the disco finishes, Clare is ready for bed but Jill wants to keep dancing. They have a row and Jill goes off with Rod, a Politics fresher, who wears red corduroy flares into which he stows (so it's rumoured) a huge cock. She doesn't return that night and it's three years before Jill and Clare talk properly again.

Clare's single room is cold, so reluctantly she sidles into the common room where John Travolta is telling Olivia Newton John she's the one that he wants. Several Party Sevens appear. Filling a mug with warm beer, Claire chats to Jack who graduated the year before and now teaches Science in a local comprehensive. It's tough, he tells her, but he loves working with young people and there's a good career structure for someone ambitious, like him. He has a nice smile and, unlike many of the boys on her course, talks with confidence. She goes back to his flat that night and lies about being a virgin. There was a drunken one night stand the previous June but she can't remember much, so reckons it doesn't count.

Clare hasn't a clue what to do after graduation. She doesn't want to go home and somehow, over the next few months, this translates into her applying for a place on a local teacher training course. Jack has money in the bank, is personable (Clare's mother calls him 'adorable'), and in the end it feels churlish not to agree to marry him.

Later that year, on a visit home to finalise wedding arrangements, Clare goes into town to escape her mother. She's gazing at an Ercol sideboard in the window of Debenhams. It's ugly and brooding but her mother says she needs it. She doesn't know what the hell she's meant to use it for. There's a heavy tap on her shoulder.

'How ya doing then, missus?' a familiar voice says.

Clare turns to see a tall, slender woman. Jill.

It should be awkward but too much time has passed. This person in front of her is a different version to the one she used to know: less scratchy, more smiley. Social Services pay for Jill's kids to be in a nursery one day a week, and so they end up in a trendy wine bar down by the river.

'I'm meant to be improving me life chances,' she says and arches one eyebrow in self-mockery.

'This is certainly improving how I'm seeing life. Cheers!' Clare says, raising her Pina Colada.

'You've hooked someone then.' Jill indicates Clare's sapphire and diamond engagement ring. It belonged to Jack's grandmother and apparently is very valuable.

'So it would seem. How about you?'

'Don't want to get tied down.'

'But you've got two kids, haven't you?'

'You still doing your drawing and painting stuff?'

Clare recognises Jill's old technique for avoiding answering. 'Not really. Well, a bit, you know, but what with my finals and the wedding ...'

'You should do. You was good. Anyhow, shall we have another?'

Clare looks at her watch. Her mother will be wondering where she is. 'OK, but I'll get them.'

Clare also bought the first round. Jill was always a taker, thinks Clare, but as she trips to the bar she feels happier than she has in months.

Two cocktails later Clare knows she can't marry Jack. Maybe Jill should marry him. *Jack and Jill went up the hill* ... what did they go up the hill for? She's fucked if she can remember. Jill is chatting to a bloke she met on her way back from the Ladies. She's pouting like she used to when trying to get off with someone. At one time this would have mortified Clare; now she feels exhilarated to be in the company of someone so liberated.

Late afternoon spools into evening, then later evening. Clare doesn't remember the journey home, but she has blurry recollections of Jill seeing her into a taxi. This time it's not the rose-bed she spews on but the hall carpet.

Her mother is tight-lipped when she takes her to the station on Sunday evening. She pulls into the drop off area, 'I suggest no mention is made to Jack of your unedifying performance last night. I've laundered your clothes. They're on the back seat.'

Clare mumbles her thanks. Her hangover is so severe she feels like dying. She leans over, intending to give a peck on the cheek but her mother recoils, 'You still reek of booze. Take some Mint Imperials from the glove compartment.'

As she reaches into the back to get the clothes, her mother grabs her arm, 'You're all I've got, Clare. Don't let me down.'

1977

Jill has a rule to not drink until the kids are in bed and asleep. After a heavy night, it's hard getting them up, breakfasted and off to school. Even so, she's never once failed, however shit she feels.

It's been a bad day today, though, and as soon as they're in from school she parks them in front of *The Flumps* with crisps and pop and cracks open some cans. Maybe the bitchy remark from one of the other mums in the playground about the PTA has tipped her over; or maybe it's the sheaf of unpaid bills; or the fact that the flirty guy in the offy had blanked her when she'd gone in that lunchtime. If she's honest with herself, she knows full well the cause. Her failure to get elected onto the PTA committee was discrimination. Pure and simple. Pure and fucking simple. After all these years she should be used to it, but this is directed against her girls as well as herself, and it hurts like hell. By mid-evening she manages to send the girls to their bedroom but is unable to get herself off the settee where she sprawls, wasted.

The first thing Clare sees outside Jill's basement flat is a police car, its blue lights circling. Clusters of neighbours stand on doorsteps and on the opposite pavement. She'd been to Jill's flat once before, two years ago, when she'd come to try and explain why her mother didn't want Jill included on the wedding-guest list. Jill hadn't taken it well, but tonight she is the one person Clare needs to see. To make amends, if she can.

She gets past the policeman on the door by claiming to be an old family friend. In the living room Jill is sitting on the settee, arms around her two wide-eyed daughters. Her chin is lifted in defiance, but Clare can smell her fear.

Present are a policewoman and someone Clare assumes to be a social worker.

'Neighbours reported the younger child wandering up and down the street, alone. Prior to this, both children had been heard crying for at least an hour,' the policewoman says.

'Are you under the influence of something?' asks the social worker, 'Drink? Drugs?'

'I'm so sorry I'm late, Jill. I know I said I'd be here an hour ago to look after the girls,' Clare wades in, adopting the assertive and brisk tone she's heard her mother use so often when faced with intransigent authority. 'My fault entirely, officer, if there's been any misunderstanding. It was my mother's funeral today and, as I'm sure you'll understand, I completely lost track of time. But I'm here now, so there's nothing at all to be concerned about. We don't want to waste your time and I'm sure nobody wants unnecessary amounts of form-filling. I'm going to make us all some food, then it's bathtime and bed for these two young ladies.'

When the policewoman and social worker have gone, Jill doesn't thank her. But then again Clare doesn't expect her to.

Jack's never hit Clare. The occasional shove, her arm held too tightly, but nothing that you could really call violence. The trouble is, she spends a lot of her time trying to avoid annoying him: not moaning about her classes, not smoking on the patio, keeping her art materials in the shed. He's a deputy head now and constantly complains about getting landed with all the crap. When he's made head, he promises, everything will change: they will buy a bigger house and she'll be able to cut down her teaching hours. Clare only does three mornings a week as it is and can't see the point of getting a bigger place just for the two of them. Babies aren't going to happen now, and less teaching is more time spent alone. She's thought of leaving him and has even broached the subject. Each time Jack has appeared shocked and apologised for his grumpiness, promising holidays and talking her round, just like he always can.

Arriving home after work, she kicks off her shoes and has a big glass of White Zin – straight from the fridge, lovely and cold. Often she'll have another couple of glasses, maybe more, but they never match the hit of that first one. She's likely to doze off in the afternoons and always sets an alarm so that she is awake in good time before Jack's arrival. She replaces the bottle in the fridge with a new one and hides the empty bottle in a case at the bottom of her wardrobe. Then she cleans her teeth.

One evening she and Jack are watching the late news: Jack's marking and she's slumped in the armchair, trying to think up an excuse to go outside on a cold January evening. Suddenly she sits bolt upright. Jill is at the front of a small group of demonstrators being interviewed outside the Old Bailey, where it's just been announced that the Birmingham

Six have failed in their latest appeal. Jill has a new look: short spiky red hair, like Annie Lennox, and she's dressed in a man's pin-striped jacket with a tartan scarf encircling her slender neck. She's articulate and measured in her comments, yet Clare still detects that familiar don't-fuck-with-me glint in her eye.

'I knew her.'

Jack looks up, 'Really? Sounds like a troublemaker. It's obvious those Irish bastards did it. They should stay locked up for life.'

Clare hasn't the energy to disagree, 'She was certainly a troublemaker. But we got on.' An image of the last time she saw Jill swims into her head: Jill with her arms around her two girls, her hair in wild corkscrews, her face creased and blotched. Yet still beautiful.

'I can't imagine what you had in common,' Jack mutters.

Clare waits until Jack is asleep then creeps downstairs. She trips over some shoes and falls heavily onto the parquet floor, grazing both her palms. Panting, she stays on all fours until confident that Jack's not stirred. She hauls herself up, gets the key to the back door and slowly unlocks it, trying to avoid a click. She waits again once the door is unlocked and again when she opens it. Still no sound. Outside it's hard not to run up the long path to the shed and she wills herself to take it slowly. She hasn't got a torch but it's a route she can now do blindfolded. The vodka is hidden in a carton under the work bench, the bottle covered with her watercolour materials, which she regularly pretends to have used by wetting the brushes and re-arranging the paints and canvases. A pulse in Clare's groin flickers at the prospect of the sharp, clean liquid running down her throat and entering her system. It's almost sexual, this obsessive desire to prove to herself that she's still alive.

1995

Jill's memoir *Courting Trouble* goes to the top of the best-seller list. She appears on *The Time, The Place* and on the front covers of *Vogue* and *Rolling Stone*. A striking single mother of mixed race from a troubled background, who rose to become one of the country's top lawyers specialising in high-profile social justice cases: it's not difficult to see why the media love her. She's completely open about her alcohol dependency when younger, and in one chapter describes with brutal honesty how she almost lost her children. It was only the intervention of the woman she calls Friend C who stopped Social Services taking any action. *The influence of the articulate middle class*, she writes, *made me realise the power of words. It turned my life around. I've not had a drink since.* At the book launch one interviewer asks if she's still in touch with Friend C. *Sadly not. In the end we each chose to go our separate ways.* Another enquires if she is happy. *Happy?* she laughs, *What's happy?*

2000

Jack doesn't divorce Clare immediately after the accident. He waits, choosing the dawn of the new millennium to initiate proceedings. The irony is that in spite of having virtually no sight in one eye, she now paints a lot. She was lucky to have escaped with her life from the fire in the shed (a dropped ciggy, Jack always claims, though she doesn't remember smoking that night). Sitting in the garden, drink in one hand and brush in the other, Clare paints canvas after canvas: frenzied sunsets that are red swirls of Rioja, cornfields that flow like frothy cider into a glass and flowers, zings of amber, firing through her veins like shots of whisky.

Buying It Back

by Louis de Bernières

Near the beginning of my writing career, when I found myself living in London and on the 1990s Best of Young British list, and everybody thought I was young and hot and up-and-coming, I suddenly began to be invited to literary parties. There was still a budget for having fun in those days, and publishing hadn't been taken over by women in their thirties who were interested in being healthy and sensible and politically correct. Lady publishers back then liked their loucheness and boozy nights and big lunches as much as their male counterparts. Just as much was achieved by these reprobates as is achieved nowadays by their more sober successors. My publisher used to fly everybody over to Amsterdam, annually. This came to an end allegedly because of worries about the carbon footprint, but it was really because the puritans always win in the end. If there had not been a good reason to end the frolics, the puritans would have invented one. And if the puritans didn't always win, we'd have no good old days to look back on, would we? Now that they really have gone, and our little age of Dionysus and his Bacchantes is only a tender memory, writers who want to carouse have to invite their friends around and do it at home, at their own expense.

Alexandra Pringle, a sparkly and beautiful woman, now at Bloomsbury, was a great party-goer, and I think it was to one of her parties that I went, somewhere in north London. It was not an area I knew well, as I had only lived in very down-at-heel places, such as Brixton and Archway, and Raynes Park.

I had not bothered to eat anything, as I had assumed

there would be nibbles. There weren't however; there was just a huge quantity of heavy duty New World wine, the kind of Merlot and Shiraz that is 14% alcohol, rich and fruity beyond reason, and the only kind of wine that makes me feel seriously ill, as I was shortly to discover.

I tucked into the wine, and felt perfectly all right. There was a young woman there who, I had been reliably informed, fancied me like crazy. She was pretty and personable, but I had never fancied her, and so I had kept my distance in order not to be hurtful. Even so, after a few glasses I put my arm around her waist and became affectionate. She seemed to freeze a little, as if she knew I was only wearing wine goggles, and then, as I stood there with my arm around her waist and a glass of Australian hyperwine in my left hand, I suddenly knew with absolute certainty that I really had to leave.

I put down my glass, ran downstairs, and grabbed my hat and coat. Outside, the freezing midnight air hit me with a delicious and welcome shock, and I began to walk briskly home.

After a few miles I realized that I had no idea where I was, and that it was in any case probably impossible to walk from North London to Wandsworth in a reasonable amount of time. I sat on the low wall of a cemetery, and began to feel confused and ill. Despite the freezing air, I broke out into a sweat.

I had had two decades of being as poor as a church mouse, and had never hailed a London taxi before. I had never even stayed in a hotel. I remember Esther Freud telling me I was crazy to persist in using the underground when I wasn't poor any more. On this night, I realized I would have to hail a taxi, and damn the expense.

When a taxi appeared, I got in, and all seemed well. But then the driver began to talk and talk and talk and talk.

If you have had too much Australian wine, the last thing you want is to have to concentrate on listening to somebody talk and talk and talk and talk. The effort of concentration soon made me feel sick, and then more sick, until the waves of nausea became almost too much to resist. I think my voice must have become thicker, and my misery transparent.

Suddenly the driver glanced in his rearview mirror, and said, 'You're gonna be sick, aren't you, mate? You're not gonna be sick in my car.'

He stopped the taxi, got out, went and opened the boot, and came back with a large rubber bucket, that he presented to me, saying, 'You be sick in that.'

I vomited into the rubber bucket, just about as far as Vauxhall, and after that I felt a great deal better, even though the driver was still talking at the same relentless pace. When we arrived at my address on Garratt Lane, I said, 'What shall we do about the bucket?' whereupon he replied, 'Either you go in and wash it out, and I leave the meter running, or you buy the bucket.'

I looked at it with the expert eye of someone who used to be a hard landscape gardener. It was a pukka bucket, good and solid, a high quality black bucket, with a thick galvanised wire loop and a nicely turned wooden handle. It would easily cope with a full load of pug. I could just see myself building a stone wall with a trowel and that superb bucket's loyal support. I said, 'How much is the bucket?' and he said, 'Two quid.'

I looked at it with a sense of wonder. A pukka bucket like that was surely worth a lot more. In fact, it was an irresistible bargain. I said, 'I'll buy the bucket.'

Once indoors I poured the regurgitated Merlot and Shiraz down the loo, and then abruptly had to sit on it myself. Afterwards I felt like the woman in that old Platex girdle advert, back in the black and white days, who alleg-edly felt five pounds thinner for the wearing of it.

The bucket did die in the end, but for many years it served me well. After I moved to Norfolk I used to let it fill with rainwater, and my pet rook Wutput would splash happily in it for hours. It was just exactly the right size for a rook bath, and Wutput splashing in the bucket under the garage downpipe is one of my happiest memories. Her delight was touching and immense.

Now that the parties are all over, and I am cold and up-and-going, and not even on the Best of Old British list, I only drink subtle red wines, such as Beaujolais and Pinot Noir. I do sometimes wonder how many other people bought a bucket of their own vomit back in the nineties.

I still hate Merlot and Shiraz, viscerally, and in the true sense of that word; with my very guts.

Waiting for the Men

by Bethan Roberts

They were waiting for the men to return from their Christmas do, and it was going to be a long afternoon. Puckering her lips, Pat aimed a thin column of smoke towards her sister Jenny's kitchen window. It had started to snow around lunchtime, and the flakes were still falling, kissing the panes and settling on the crooked birdbath and the hedge outside.

Jenny handed Pat a glass decorated with a transfer of hunters and their dogs, then inched away from the cigarette. Jenny had always been better behaved, neater, and softer-spoken than her sister. But Pat was the one who'd bagged the better-looking husband.

Pat sucked the last dregs from her cigarette and exhaled as slowly as she could. After this one, she was giving up. She ground out her final fag in Jenny's sink and left the butt in the plughole, ash bleeding onto the wet stainless steel.

Jenny was too busy checking her mince pies to notice. 'Did Bob say what time they were starting?' she asked.

'Round eleven.' Pat downed her sherry. 'It'll be full swing by now.'

'Richard's no good with lunchtime drinking,' said Jenny.

All the men worked at the local car factory. Jenny's husband Richard was a foreman. Pat's husband Bob and her youngest son Mark were on the shop floor. This would be Mark's first Christmas work do, but it was Bob whom Pat was worried about.

'Richard's driving back, though, isn't he?' she said. 'And he's always been more sensible than Bob –'

'I'm not sure that's true.'

'That's why he's the boss.'

'Richard is not the boss,' said Jenny, gouging hot pies from the tin with a knife. 'And he should've left the car at home.'

'I wouldn't, if I had a new Escort,' Pat said.

Jenny arranged the pies on a plate, then scattered caster over the top. 'Won't your Mark keep an eye on Bob?' she asked. 'Didn't you have a word?'

Pat laughed. 'My word counts for nothing. They'll just egg each other on.'

Jenny raised her eyebrows.

'What?' Pat asked.

'Nothing.'

Pat knew what her sister was thinking: *you should have more control over your men*. In the summer, Bob had blacked out at the factory and, when he came round, he was ranting about being blind. By lunchtime, though, he could see again, and everyone on the shop floor had ribbed him about coming to work pissed. Pat had insisted he see the doctor, who said it might have been a mini-stroke. He'd advised Bob to take it easy; cut back on the drinking, and certainly stop smoking. Bob had done neither of these things. Pat's decision to give up the fags was an attempt to show him it was possible to try to break an addiction. But she knew that what she did made little difference to him.

'They'll be absolutely bloody plastered,' said Pat. 'Not that I care.'

Jenny held out the plate of pies. Pat snatched one and bit into it. Scalding mincemeat scoured her tongue. She held a hand to her mouth, and Jenny passed her another sherry to douse the fire.

'You should be more careful,' she said.

It was what their mother, Nelly, said, all the time.

*

Pat and Jenny carried the sherry and mince pies into the front room. Nelly was stationed in the wide armchair by the window, her feet swelling over the edges of her slippers like pie crusts. Jenny's Jack Russell lay dozing by the gas fire, giving off a gluey odour. Pat and Jenny sat on the sofa, and they all jiggled the hot pies from finger to finger and dusted crumbs from their chests.

Outside, snow was still falling as the sky darkened, and children, released from their last day of school, began to appear in the street.

'Bugger,' said Nelly. 'That's that, then. Peace shattered.'

Although her only child, Sean, was now fifteen, Jenny leapt to the window to watch for him. Pat noticed her sister's face lighten as she spotted him and waved, and her neck prickled with jealousy. It had been years since she'd felt anything like delight at the prospect of a son of hers coming home. And now that Mark spent every hour of the working day in his father's company, neither of them seemed to notice Pat very much. They left for work; they returned and cleared their plates; they escaped to different pubs.

The three women listened to Sean opening the back door, tossing his bag to the floor, and rooting in the fridge.

'There's mince pies in here,' Jenny called.

He appeared in the sitting room. He was gangly, with oversized glasses that he had a habit of pushing up his nose with one finger, like a much older person. He kissed his grandmother's head, then pecked his mother's cheek and reached for a pie.

'Hello, Aunty Pat,' he said, through a mouthful of crumbs. He flopped down next to her on the sofa, but no kiss was offered.

'So what's Father Christmas bringing *you*, young man?' she asked, unsure whether her tone was flirtatious, and, if it was, whether that was all right. When he was younger,

Sean used to blush when she called him *the handsome boffin*, and she'd enjoyed his embarrassment.

'I don't believe in Father Christmas any more,' he said.

'Ssh!' said Pat. 'Don't let your mum hear that.'

Jenny pulled a sad face. 'Every day he finds new ways to break my heart.'

'Rubbish!' said Pat. 'He's perfect.'

'Almost,' said Jenny, with a smile that was warmly returned by her son.

Pat's throat tightened. Christmas hadn't been the same since her boys grew up. The eldest two had left home a couple of years ago, and she knew it wouldn't be long before Mark followed. The best time had been when she'd saved for weeks and got Mark that Evel Knievel toy from the club book. It hadn't worked as it should – the wheelies lasted less than a second, and it never jumped further than a few inches – but Mark had loved it. He'd slept with Evel every night for a full year.

'How long have we got,' asked Nelly, 'until the bomb goes off?'

Pat glanced at her watch. 'I'd say it'll be at least two hours till they're back.'

Nelly reached for the bottle of Harvey's Bristol Cream and refilled their glasses.

'Can I have one?' asked Sean.

Jenny hesitated, so Pat leapt in. 'Go on, love. It's Christmas.'

Sean looked at his mother, who said, 'Just one.'

'This your first?' asked Pat, pouring.

Sean gave a giggle. 'Course it is, Aunty Pat.'

'It had better be,' said Jenny.

Pat rolled her eyes at Sean as she handed him his glass. Then she clinked hers against his. 'Here's to waiting for the men.'

They both drank. Pat did her best not to laugh when Sean made a self-consciously dramatic performance of coughing and spluttering, presumably to convince his mother that the sherry was indeed his first ever alcoholic drink. She allowed the looseness in her legs to travel up her spine, then focused on the Christmas tree, not as large as the one in her own house, but, she had to admit, much prettier. The fairy lights were evenly spaced along the plastic branches, and wasn't it so much better to stick to silver tinsel only? No doubt Sean had helped his mother with the decoration. Pat's own effort featured great wodges of multicoloured twinkle stuck at the top, and bare branches at the bottom. The overall effect was a sort of crazed clumpiness.

She slumped back on the sofa.

'You're not drunk, are you, Aunty Pat?' Sean asked.

'Not half as drunk as them men'll be!' said Nelly, delightedly.

'So I'm interested,' said Sean, 'in your predictions about the *scale* of drunkenness. Do you think they'll have already vomited by the time they come home, or will they save that for, you know, the moment they cross the threshold?'

'Sean!' Jenny warned.

'Because last Christmas, if I remember correctly, Uncle Bob puked on our hedge.'

'He *aimed* for the bin,' said Pat.

'Missed it, though.'

'He was drunk.'

'My point exactly.'

Nelly laughed and refilled her glass. She'd unbuttoned her collared cardigan, and her soft chins trembled. 'Do you remember that time I fell into Richard's hedge? Oh, he *was* cross! That was your Bob's fault.'

'Richard wasn't cross,' Jenny said. 'He was just worried about you –'

'Bob kept feeding me that punch you made, Jenny – lovely, it was, tasted like cherryade – and then I got up and *whoops!*'

'There was a Gran-shaped hole in dad's prize shrubbery,' said Sean.

'What time is it?' Pat asked.

'Four-thirty,' said Jenny.

'They'll be locked in the Magic Midget by now,' said Nelly.

'A fate worse than death,' said Sean.

The dog gave a wheeze and twitched awake, momentarily lifting its head. After casting its sad eyes over them, it yawned and went back to sleep.

'Still snowing,' said Sean, going to the window.

Pat joined him, and had to place a steadying hand on top of the telly. 'Maybe we'll get snowed in,' she said.

'Don't!' said Jenny. 'I haven't got all my bits for Christmas dinner yet.'

'We can have Bacon Grill and sardines,' said Sean. 'Like in the war.'

'Weren't no Bacon Grill in the war,' said Nelly.

Jenny came to the window, and they all stared at the snow. It was coming down thickly; the road was already completely white. While she was watching the flakes whirl past, Sean ducked behind his mother and attempted to pour himself another drink, but Pat stopped him. 'Don't,' she said, a hand on his wrist. 'Don't be like the others.'

He considered her through his spectacles. His eyes were flecked with yellow, and deep-set, like his father's. She could see nothing of her own family in him, which gave her hope.

'We'll have a white Christmas,' he said.

'It'll all be gone by then,' said Pat.

*

Two hours later, with the snow still coming down, Sean suggested he go out to look for the men.

'But your dad's got the car,' said Jenny. 'He's probably driving back now.'

'That's what I'm worried about,' Sean muttered.

Jenny's face hardened.

Although her sister hadn't breathed a word to her about it, Pat knew from Bob that Richard had recently been stopped for drink driving, and had got off with a warning.

'Don't be silly!' Jenny said, recovering herself and patting Sean's hand. 'You can't go out. You haven't even had any tea yet!'

No-one had eaten anything but mince pies. Jenny looked at the crumbs on the empty plate, but she didn't move. Sean removed his hand from his mother's.

With the gas fire turned up to max, Nelly and the dog were both snoring now.

'Do you think the car will start OK, though?' asked Pat.

'It's a new Escort,' said Jenny. 'Of course it will start OK.'

Pat noticed her sister's words were slightly slurred, and her cheeks were flushed.

'Surely he won't be able to drive in this,' Pat said.

Jenny waved a hand across her face. 'Richard drives in anything.' Then she sank into the sofa and closed her eyes. 'He'd drive on *water*, if I let him.'

Pat checked her watch. It was quarter to seven. 'I think I'll make us a coffee,' she said.

Sean followed Pat through to the kitchen, where it was much colder. While the kettle boiled, Pat thought about her husband and son, out there. If they were walking, the snow would slow them down, cool the alcohol in their veins. It would sober them up, too, and make them glad to get back. But would their limbs, already turned to jelly by the booze, be able to carry them home? What if Bob blacked out again?

Sean helped himself to some ham from the fridge, eating several slices straight from the waxed paper. Then he tipped a bottle of milk to his mouth.

Snapping off the kettle, Pat said, 'I'm fed up with this waiting. Let's go and look for them.'

Sean wiped his mouth with the back of his hand. 'Mum won't like it.'

'This is Abingdon, not Alaska. We can wrap up warm.'

He cast a look at her feet. 'You'll be OK in those?'

The pixie boots had been an impulse buy. She'd seen schoolgirls coming home in these suede booties with vaguely Indian tassels swinging from the cuffs. With their low heel and rounded toes, they looked like shoes you could walk anywhere in.

'I'll be fine,' she said.

*

Neither spoke as they trudged along the snowy pavement. Pat couldn't remember the last time she'd walked in such bad weather. The freezing wind blasted her face, making her eyes water. She pulled on her gloves and shoved her hands deep into her pockets.

It was dark now, and there was no traffic, no kids; they had the quiet street all to themselves. As they walked, the snowy road before them was weirdly illuminated by the street lamps' orange glow, making it look like the kind of smooth carpet you saw on *Dynasty*.

The Magic Midget was about a mile away. When they reached the stream near the school, Sean glanced back the way they'd came. 'Mum'll be worrying by now,' he said.

'You're fifteen! She needs to stop treating you like a child.'

They stopped on the tiny bridge and peered down into the shallow water, taking a moment to watch it ripple across stones, crisp packets, weeds and empty beer bottles. It was strange to see something else that was moving, something that wasn't held down by snow.

'Did you used to come here with my boys?' Pat asked.

Sean leaned over the railing so far that Pat had to stop herself from grabbing his duffel.

'They used to push me in,' he said, still half-dangling over the bridge. 'And shove the sticklebacks they'd caught down my pants.'

Pat laughed.

'It's not funny,' Sean said, his voice cracking. He straightened up, and she saw his pink, serious face, his glasses speckled with snow. He wasn't shorter than her boys, but he was skinnier, and she realised that the way he stood – shoulders wilting and toes pointing together – made him appear slight. She remembered how often her boys had seemed to loom over him when they were younger. Back then, she'd thought Jenny ridiculously over-protective. She'd used the phrase *boys will be boys*, and had agreed when Bob expressed his opinion that Sean needed to toughen up.

Sean snatched off his glasses, then scrubbed away the tear on his cheek.

A pulse of shame went through Pat's body with such force that she had to steady her breathing. A moment passed before she managed to say, 'They all wanted to be like their father. And I never told them not to.'

He sniffed. None of Pat's boys had cried since they were toddlers. Mark had had an especially keening grizzle; it used to go on and on, drilling into her skull. She remembered one night, when Bob had been working and she'd been alone, Mark had started. He must have been almost three years old. Every time she'd coaxed him back to sleep he'd woken within minutes and begun crying again. In the end, she'd charged into his room. It was as if her body were an engine fuelled by rage. She'd grabbed his shoulders, got up close to his little face and yelled right into it: *Will you just shut the fuck up?* She'd never hit her boys, but she'd come close to walloping Mark that night. He was stunned into silence, but as she'd left the room he'd cried out in a thin and wavering voice, 'Somebody help me, please!'

That voice was so wounded, so terrified, so utterly alone. It had stopped her dead. Her boy was calling for help from someone – anyone – else. In that moment, Pat had felt as if she'd done the worst thing a mother could do: she'd abandoned her son.

'I'm so sorry, Sean,' she said.

Sean wiped a hand across his face. 'I can't see in these,' he said, holding up his glasses and trying to smile. 'I need windscreen wipers or something.'

Pat held out her arm. 'Let me guide you, then.'

He looked down. 'You're shivering,' he said.

'I'm bloody freezing, that's all.'

He nodded and took hold of her sleeve.

They ploughed on over the bridge, towards the school. In her flimsy pixie boots, Pat's feet were soaked now, and her toes felt iced together; but it seemed important to go on, even though she knew she was clinging to Sean as much as he was clinging to her, and if she were to go down she might take him with her.

*

They heard them before they saw them. Bob's voice, singing 'Let It Snow,' rang out across the deserted main road. Pat stopped beneath the willow at the school gates and listened. Mark was joining in, and they didn't sound at all bad. Bob had always sung well; he liked to mention that he'd once been a choirboy. 'Picture it. Me, in a smock,' he'd say.

Bob and Mark came into view. In the snow their edges looked blunted, as if they were a child's partially-erased drawing. They were swaying together. Mark was clutching Bob's shoulder, and Bob had his palm on the top of his son's head. It was difficult to tell if they were using each other for ballast or pushing each other away.

Unlike Bob and Mark, Richard was wearing a scarf, but he was singing, too. With his arms stretched wide and his head thrown back, he was belting out the bit about being *warm all the way home.*

Pat pulled Sean back into the shadow of the willow's branches. 'Let's listen to the sweet sound of the choir,' she whispered.

Sean giggled.

Led by Bob, the men progressed from 'Let it Snow' to 'Agadoo', complete with actions. Richard was so absorbed by pushing a pineapple that he marched right into Bob, sending him flying into Mark. There was a series of loud curses, and then there was a heap of three bodies on the road. It looked as though Bob was at the bottom of the pile.

For a moment, everything was quiet. The heap of bodies was still. The snow came down. A sick feeling welled in Pat's stomach. She imagined Bob blacked out, blinded.

She was about to break cover and run to him when she heard his voice. He was yelling at his son to get off his bloody leg. Richard was standing, dusting himself off, but the other two men seemed unable to prise themselves from the snow's grip. Every time one of them got halfway upright, he was pulled down by the other. Richard went down again, and Pat heard Mark's wail. It was not the keening cry he'd had as a toddler, but a booming howl of pain that he quickly twisted into a shout of mirth.

'I think they're OK,' Sean said. 'They're laughing.'

Pat closed her eyes and exhaled. 'I don't know why we bloody bothered,' she said. 'They never need my help.'

She turned, leaving Sean beneath the tree, and hurried away, skidding slightly in the snow.

She should have known that the booze would numb both her husband and her son to any sensation at all, even pain. She tried to light a cigarette, but her fingers were stiff with cold, and the matches in her pocket were too damp to spark. She wanted only to return to Jenny's, to more mince pies and her mother's soft chins and the dog dozing by the gas fire. She could have another sherry and laugh about the stupidity of it all with her sister. 'Sean's on his way back, with his dad,' she'd explain. 'Your Richard's always been the sensible one. Of course he didn't drive! He was even wearing his scarf.'

Sean called to her to wait, but Pat didn't look back. The further she got, the more determined she was to make it alone. To think she'd been worried about those bloody idiots! Let them all freeze to death.

On the bridge, with the wind biting her skin and the snow battering her cheeks, she paused to try to light up again.

That was when Sean caught up with her. He'd put his glasses back on and he wiped at them with one gloved finger. 'Mum told me you were giving up the fags,' he said.

'Did you see them?' asked Pat, unable to mask her rage. She was still trying to strike a flame from the soggy match. 'Christ's sake! They were *laughing*.'

Sean blinked. Then he said, 'It was sort of funny.'

Pat threw the useless match into the stream.

'Did you see how hard your uncle went down?' she said. 'He should have been crying.'

She grabbed another match from the box and tried to strike it. It snapped. She swore. When would they ever learn? When would she? Tomorrow, the men would talk about how hilarious it all was, and hide their bruises beneath long sleeves and driving gloves.

Sean sighed. 'Boys don't cry, Aunty Pat.'

'You do,' she said.

He bit his lip. She hoped he might shed another tear. Maybe then she'd be able to put her arms around him, comfort him, and somehow make amends for her sons' pushing him in the stream all those years ago. But instead he raised his chin and said, 'So let's go back and check on them.'

'They're grown men. They won't want that.'

'Who cares?' Sean asked. 'I mean, really? Who the hell cares?'

Pat thought about that night when she'd yelled into Mark's little face. She knew it hadn't really been the turning point, the point at which her son had ceased to be hers and had instead followed his father and brothers into that place where women were not welcome. But now, standing on the bridge with her nephew, she wondered if she could have done more to make her own sons different. Perhaps she could have shown them some other way, before it was too late.

She dropped her unlit cigarette to the ground, where it was swallowed by snow.

Her nephew was holding out his hand. 'Come on,' he said.

Pat took it, and together they walked through the snow, stumbling now and then but never falling, back to the men.

The Bottle and the Trowel

by Laurie Cusack

You've got to hear this, Jerry! I was in the laundrette this morning staring at my washing, wondering why people seem so up-tight over here. Look at the loonie-goons, you'd always say, with that twisted smile plastered across your mug. Remember that first day we hopped on the bus and the tube, Jerry? That mad sprint to work; green to the bone; carrying all our kit; lost in the bowels of London; creasing up with the laughing; bumping in to all those shams.

Fresh off the boat, weren't we, sham? Clueless. London's a bastard of a place sometimes…

Those two dossers were in the laundrette again, Jerry. They were hugging the machines for warmth, god love them. And they were half way to pissey heaven at 10 o'clock in the shagging morning.

Latchicos, you whispered in my ear, when we did our first wash in there. A stain on our nation, Lorcan. I loved the piss-taking way you said that. You sounded like the Taoiseach. Sure, they're harmless enough, I whispered back to you. We're only one pay cheque away from living in this laundrette ourselves. Life was a *gas* back then, wasn't it, Jerry? Now I realise there's millions who're only a cheque or two away from the street.

Anyway, you'd not blame those dossers today, sham. If ye had a heart at all, that is. It's perishing out there. It would snap the bones off ye, so it would, as they say back home. The cement was freezing on the trowel yesterday. The *yellow jacket brigade* kept looking at the thermometer. But it was only for show. The job's way behind, sham! They're bending all the rules, now. Remember how strict they were at the beginning, hey?

I'm still sending bits of money back to me Ma and the *quare* one.

'Lorcan, you're as soft as shit.'

Did you just speak, sham. Are you smirking, Jerry?

Wheeze, wheeze, wheeze...

The sound of your ventilator still freaks me out.

Staring into the dirty suds this morning got me thinking about Achill. How desperate things are back there. All us young bucks splitting. You can't eat mountains, can you? You said that to me once. And you were dead on. There's nothing in that place, now. Nothing.

Wake up, Jerry! Tell me to shut the feck up. I'm missing you, ye bollix.

That dinky nurse, who was in here, five minutes ago. The one with braided hair, what a *dolly*. She's got a cracking smile, so she has. She says I need to talk to you like this, as much as I can. *He needs to hear talk from people he knows. It's crucial*, she says. Well I felt a bit stupid at the start, with this talking malarkey, Jerry. But that *dolly* keeps encouraging me every time she comes in to check on your ventilator, or calibrate it – or whatever else she does. I still clam up when she's about, though. She's ever so flirty, Jerry. She seems to like ye. *Keep talking to him as normal as you can. Speak to him as if nothing's happened*, she keeps saying. It's hard, though, Jerry. Hard. I still can't get used to seeing you like this, sham. All these tubes and wires you're connected to – does my head in, so it does.

Sorry...

I'm trying to tell you how it is...

Top-notch staff, over here, Jerry. I'll say that for it.

Wheeze, wheeze, wheeze...

The bankers have been let off the hook, Lorcan. They're thieving gobshites, the lot of them, simple as. You said that to me, Jerry, when we started that Hackney job. If it was the likes of you or me we'd have been flogged, flayed and banged up for life. We were thrown to the dogs, weren't we? Collateral damage. I didn't see it back then. No wonder there's so many Irish piss-heads roaming this town like lost wildebeests.

The dossers went to a different level, this morning, Jerry. You'd have loved it. Things move fast in London, don't they, sham?

I love the pong of powder in that laundrette. You sit in there with the weekend ahead of you and it calms your nerve-ends. I know it sounds daft, but it's kind of soothing. And the drivel from the dossers can be entertaining as well. But this morning was mental. I'll have a go at doing their voices for ye, Jerry. Their patter was mad, so it was.

'Thunderbird wine's the tipple of tipples, Mick-Mack.'

'What ye on about, Bert, ye bampot.'

'Getting the fucker is the hard bit. I had to walk miles to get this. My tootsies are fucking killing me.'

'Plenty of choice out there, Bert, why get zonked on one brand?'

Is that realistic enough for ye, sham? They were at each other's throats. It was a gas, you'd have creased.

I'll paint the picture for ye, Jerry. That Mick-Mack fella's as bog-Irish as they come, a solid lump of skin. You called him ox-man, didn't ye? Those purple thread veins in his brick-red face, like you'd see in an old road map. His mop of wild hair's still crying out for a groom. Remember when we tried to get a fix on his accent and I was willing to put shillings down that he hailed from Kerry and you swore blind that he had a Sligo lilt. All his years on the booze have pickled him through and through. We both agreed on that, though. Sure his ox-mug could be oiled into a masterpiece if it caught the eye of a prowling artist, Lorcan, I remember you saying, in your whiny mock TV voice, as we necked a few pints in The Rose and Crown. You should be on stage, ya bolix! Oh, the laughter was on us, then. Their silly-slobber cracked us up. We vowed we'd never end up like them, no matter what this town threw at us – ye remember that, don't ye?

You should have seen me necking those shots last night. I was in The Bell with a gang from the site – acting the eejit. Showing off, so I was. It's more to do with your mangled self, Jerry, boy. More like I was trying to drink it out of my mind. Maybe trying to talk it out like this is a wee bit better. To think I was gassing to you about the Man U game as you passed blocks out to me on the scaffolding. It could have been me. That's what keeps jarring me mind, Jerry. Your shriek is on playback 24/7 – that sound of splintering board still fucks my head up. The thud of everything hitting the deck in one mighty *vapumph*. It shook the building, raised a mighty cloud of dust, so it did. You poor sod. We told them that MDF was fucked, as well, but they still made us stack the bricks and concrete blocks on it. I'll never forget the mad scramble to get the stuff off of ye. Now the bastards want me to lie about the board. They want me to sign a fecking form. Cunts.

All of this was rumbling in me mind, Jerry, as I was getting my clothes ready for the dryer. I could still hear the dossers blubbering away in the background, as well, mind you.

'Thunderbird is the mother of all wines, comrade.'

'I've told ye, don't fucking comrade me, ye blackguard.'

'Some days you want me to call you comrade.'

'Well, today's the *fecking* day I don't.'

'Maybe I'm a slave to taste, Mick-Mack.'

'A thirst for the exotic, hey, *hey?*'

'If you say so.'

'*I don't say ... he says!* The MESSIAH says! How many times do ye have to be told, ye twerp.'

'What are you on about now?'

'Are ye deaf as well as stupid?'

'Don't start going weird on me, Mick-Mack.'

'Give us a swig, ye Philistine cunt.'

'That machine doesn't work, me old flower,' the one called Bert shouted across at me, Jerry. He always looks twitchy and ready to dart, remember? We'd seen him zipping about the place. You said, he's on booze business, Lorcan. You said it in your David Attenborough voice. We were coming back from a shift. Both of us sitting in the King's seat on the top deck of the 53b bus. He's still wearing that same shit-up tweed jacket that shines with grime. And his filthy canvas knapsack's still slung on his back.

'Thanks, pal,' I shouted across at him.

You'd have said, the lunatics are running the asylum now, Lorcan. They were really on form today.

I'll have another go at their voices for ye, Jerry.

'I love the look of it, Mick-Mack. There's something about its name that I'm –'

'Give me a slug, cunt-face.'

'A working man's wine, this is.'

'American loony juice, you mean, brewed to keep us down, that's what this piss is for, ye old fart.'

'Now don't be like that about me favourite tipple, comrade.'

'I'll stick this in ya face if ye call me that again, ya *fecking* wind-up merchant.'

I looked across at Mick-Mick to see if it was banter. I wasn't sure, Jerry. He looked edgy. Things kick off so easily in this town, don't they? Anyway, I pushed a load of 20p coins in to the spin dryer. The clicking of buttons on the glass door and the rumble of the machine triggered more thoughts of money, rent and food. The struggle to keep it all going: I'm homesick to fuck, to tell ye the god's honest truth. All this was bubbling in my mind. And when you think things can't get any worse that's when they usually do…

I'll try and put me best drunken slur on, for this bit, Jerry.

'Thought you were into revolutionary stuff and all that blah, blah, blah, Mick-Mack.'

'Betrayed, that's what's fucking up, if ye really want ta fucking know.'

'By who?'

'Bosses, ye thick fuck.'

'Those bastards keep threatening me with work.'

'Jesus CHRIST Almighty, ye wouldn't work in a fecking iron lung,' Mick-Mack snorted.

'I'll drink to that!'

'And so will *fecking* I.'

I think that ox-man's had his snout in a few books, Jerry. I think we might've underestimated him, sham. Am I taking them off well enough for ye? Are you getting the gist of it?

That smarmy safety officer sidled up to me the other day, Jerry, as I was setting me profiles up. A firm's man through and through: 'Look, lad, we all know how you feel. It's agreed that there was a glitch in McLain's system, that wasn't picked up. Which has now been rectified. New stratagems are being put into place for the next build. Is that OK, my old son? I don't think recrimination is the way forward, do you?'

'Yeah, and my mate's up shit creek without a paddle. Will ye cop on for feck's sake!' I fired back at him.

He stormed off with the huff, 'You just can't talk to some people, you'll never ...' mutter, mutter, mutter, Jerry. Those *yellow fecking jacket boys* do your head in, don't they?

Then a soft union skin came into the canteen, as I was eating me scran, 'Look, Lorcan, it's not worth rocking the boat over this,' he said, in a hushed sort of a way.

I know they're shitting their knickers over the Health and Safety Executive's visit next week, Jerry. They've got wind of my bolshie mutterings around site. I should've been keeping me head down. Now they're really pressurising me to sign. What would you do, Jerry?

Hughie Cairns, my old tradesman used to slag our gaffers off to fuck: *Mushrooms, that's all we are to them. They like to keep us in the dark and feed us shit. Mushrooms.* Then he'd laugh his head off, Jerry. I learnt stacks from Hughie. *Super glue that into your mind, gosser,* he'd say, as we pointed our brickwork up. Hughie would have seen this coming a mile off.

I don't want them to get away with this, I really don't, but the way things are...

It kicked off, big time, Jerry! The dryer was winding down from its cycle when Mick-Mack went ballistic. Straight out of the blue, he started going ape-shit. Mad. You'd have loved it.

'*Ahhhhh* ... HE'S DYING FOR US EVERY DAY, DO YEE NOT KNOW?' That mental *fecker* started screaming his head off.

I nearly jumped out my my skin, sham.

He was staring right at me. I was feeling dog rough myself. I looked at him across the aisle and he'd gone as rigid as a standing-stone. The lava-red face on him was blazing. He looked as mad as fuck. It looked like some sort of fit, Jerry. Then his body started jerking a bit before he took a few steps towards me. He kept slugging at the dregs in the bottle. He gripped that Thunderbird bottle like a baton as if he was conducting his own orchestra. I was twitching a bit as the crazy *fecker* came towards me.

'His blood's dripping on the whole world,' he squealed at me like an old pig in the queue for slaughter. He was in a bad way, Jerry.

'On your fucking knees, heathen,' he yelled at me.

He was having a vision, I swear to ye, Jerry.

He looked mad enough for a section. His index finger was pointing at me, all his focus was trained on me, as if I was the devil in his crazy episode.

'Gaffers have sucked all the goodness out of me. I'll tell you that for naff all, gossoon,' he hissed at me. It felt like he was reading my fecking mind, sham.

He kept eye-balling me. A mad paddy preacher in my face. His eyes were as large as duck eggs and they were locked on to me. Saliva and snot were drooling off him. He was twisted with righteous rage, Jerry. It was pouring out of him, sure it was.

'Can't you see? The redeemer's blood is dripping on the whole world, lad.'

I thought about getting the hell out of there, Jerry. Feck the washing. I didn't want this on me day off, I wanted the hair of the dog myself, for feck's sake.

'He's dying for us every day, can't you see, heathen?'

It reminded me of people wailing and crying on some fecking mountainside, back home. I tried looking away; it was too painful to watch. He was breaking up in front of me. They'll take him away at this rate, I thought, as I watched the spittle building up on his face.

Then the lump collapsed to his knees.

'*Rejoice, rejoice, rejoice!*' he roared.

'Cool it, Mick-Mack, they'll clear us off again,' Bert

pleaded with him. 'I'll go and get some more grog.'

'I've forgot more than you'll ever know,' Mick-Mack snarled, at Bert.

'Please, Mick-Mack –'

'Look at me for fuck's sake, ye snake.'

'We'll get chucked out –'

'I've been kicked out from better places than this!'

Passers-by started looking in, Jerry.

'Bring it on, bring it on!'

It was intense, sham, intense.

'*Crucify me, crucify me, ye Philistines.*'

Is this what rock-bottom looks like? I asked myself, Jerry.

'Sinners, rejoice in the wounds of HIS majesty!'

Then something clicked in my head. Mick-Mack's babble about bosses hit home, Jerry. I'd been warned off the other day by that safety officer. That's what it was, but I didn't take much notice then, it didn't make sense: 'You'll never work in this town again, if you keep carrying on like this, me old chocolate tea pot.' That smug fucker was hinting at the 'List.' A list never entered me frigging head.

There'd been whispers about a blacklist. I'd heard about it in a pub, ages ago, but I hadn't a notion it would touch me. How these things come at you. Maybe it took what was happening in front of me at the laundrette to see what was really happening. I mean … what does a fecking blacklist mean anyway, and who the feck cares, sham? Well, what was I to think? After all, this is England, holier than holy, incorruptible, unlike shagging Ireland. That's the way I'd been thinking anyhow.

The laundrette notched up another gear, Jerry. I'll do my best with the voices, sham.

'Oi, what's this then? I've told you two,' someone shouted from outside.

Bert darted for the door at the sound of officialdom. He

zipped past Ahmed, the owner.

'I'm off, bugger ya, Mick-Mack. Sort ya fucking head out, man, if ya want to fucking drink with me again, you toss-pot,' he wheezed, on the hoof. He'd done a St. Peter on him.

I nodded at Ahmed. He always asks for ye, Jerry.

'No drinking in this place!' he shouted, as Bert flapped down the street. Then Ahmed walked up to Mick-Mack, who was still on his knees screaming:

'*Rejoice, rejoice, rejoice …*'

The business man looked vexed to fuck.

'How many times do you have to be told, you fucking ruining my place? Out, fucking … out!'

I looked across at Mick-Mack who had the faintest of smiles on his mug when he clocked Ahmed raging above him. Then the crazy fecker started singing.

Then off to reap the corn and leave where I was born
Cut a stout blackthorn to banish ghosts and goblin
Brand new pair of brogues to rattle o'er the bogs
And frighten all the dogs on the rocky road to Dublin.

What a voice. The finest of air's on him. Mick-Mack rattled it off, better than the shagging Dubliners. One Flew Over the fecking Laundrette, Jerry. Mad or what?

One, two, three, four, five
Hunt the hare and turn her down the rocky road
And all the way to Dublin, whack-fol-la-de-da.

'No Karaoke in here. Go. You must go!' Ahmed yelled down at Mick-Mack. 'I phone the police OK, go now.' He reached for his mobile.

'He's with me,' I said, as casual as a gunslinger in an old

flick. Honest to god, Jerry, that's what I said.

Ahmed froze mid finger-push. He turned and weighed me up.

'What?'

'Yeah, he's helping me with me washing.'

'You having a laugh, mate?'

'No, he's having a bad day, that's all,' I said.

And as we looked at each other, that weird night in Stockwell flashed through my mind. We'd been on the piss all day and that Achill sham tagged along with us for a while. The pain etched on that sham's face made us laugh. *The shower of fucks won't give me a start anywhere*, he kept saying. Remember him? He kept whingeing about work to us. We ended up in The Swan over in Stockwell. We were *langers*, he was one of the Gallaghers from Keem. Been over here for years. Down on his luck, so he was. He kept harping on: *I'm on this bastard of a list, so I am, lads.* We didn't take much notice. You mocked him: Another paddy on the rocks, Lorcan. Both of us cracked up, didn't we?

Ahmed kept weighing me up.

It was like *High Noon*. A shagging stand-off, sham.

'Finish your wash and get him out of here. This isn't a fucking mental hospital, it's a laundrette.' Ahmed snarled into Mick-Mack's face: 'I'm trying to run a fucking business here.' He turned and walked out.

Wheeze, wheeze, wheeze…

Jerry, oh Jerry…

Wake up, please, for *feck's* sake…

Talking it through, like this, has straightened it out for me, sham.

He's dying for us every day.

Turns out that mad-*paddy* cut through all the bullshit this morning. Because, here's you, all smashed up. And

132

here's me, thinking of signing…

They want me to be their fecking CHOCOLATE Jesus!

Feck McLain's, feck the list and feck Jesus …

Tasting Notes

by Melanie Whipman

Tom inhales leather, must, cedar, and the stale spice of perfume before the dust hits his synapses and he shudders out a volley of sneezes. He's crouched on his knees in front of Sandra's wardrobe, rifling through twenty years of her sartorial debris. He's after a clutch bag. A dark green vintage thing that he suspects is now sprayed in snot.

'Would you do me a favour?' Sandra had asked yesterday.

Tom has been in sales and marketing for years. *Would you do me a favour* is a phrase he's often used in his sales spiel. He favours it for its ability to lower the guard, open up communication, and tap into a human's innate desire to offer help. People find it difficult to say no to such a direct request, and Tom wonders when Sandra started managing him.

'Of course,' he'd replied, his voice as smooth as a Pinot Burgundy. Tom had been glad they were on the phone and she couldn't see his expression. 'What's it look like?'

'You know the one.' Sandra's voice was slightly acidic. 'You bought it at Camden Market.'

'You've got dozens of bags.' He kept his voice balanced. 'I can't remember them all.'

Tom gropes amongst the old shoe-boxes, fallen scarves, gloves, and belts, breathing in faded wafts of Sandra. Instead of the soft give of Sandra's suede bag, his fingers find something hard. A smooth glass column. He draws it out carefully. The green of the bottle is so dark it's almost black. It has the classic gold hood encasing the cork and neck. *Moët & Chandon Grand Vintage 1988.* The 1988 is inscribed in a dramatic flourish of white digits across the front of the label.

What a waste. Undrinkable now. Vintage, so a bit more longevity, but Champagne is generally short-lived. All tangy fizz and excitement at the beginning, but it's not a keeper. He slumps onto his bottom on the bedroom floor and cradles the bottle in both hands. Sandra's father bought them a case for their engagement. Ridiculously extravagant. Her side of the family always were, and he'd had a win at Chepstow. A dozen bottles. Tom thought they'd got through them all by now. But Sandra obviously kept one.

He dives back in the wardrobe and finds the bag, age-rashed and giving off a strange mix of Ysatis and mould. He takes the bottle and the bag downstairs. They sit together on the island as he scurries about unloading the dishwasher and tidying up. Not that there's much to tidy up. Without Sandra and Freya everything stays in its place. He sprays the work surfaces and wonders if Sandra will be on time and whether she'll stop for a bit. His eyes keep coming back to the Moët and the bloody clutch. He gets an ice-cooler sleeve from the freezer and shoves it over the bottle. Maybe it's still drinkable; he doesn't like waste.

Tom taps the details into his phone. It's available on a few sites. Christ, £330 for something that might not even be salvageable. He scrolls down to the description and tasting notes:

Moët & Chandon, Grand Vintage Collection 1988, the 59th in the House's history, is a dark, precise, streamlined Champagne. Disgorgement 2003.

Tom recalls the first bottle they opened. The day of their engagement party, before everyone arrived. They had no Champagne flutes back then, just an eclectic mix of those

Babycham style glasses that meant you were continually topping up your guests. And they were liable to spill. But Sandra liked the glasses. She liked all that vintage crap. Still does. No money in those days, so it was a house party with litres of plonk and some vile punch loaded with generic vodka. Asda?

That's what the green clutch bag was for. Their engagement. Tom spotted it on a stall and knew it was perfect for Sandra. Classic but edgy, with a silver clasp in the shape of a heart. It was expensive, but back then he hadn't cared, it was worth it to see her nose crease before the smile reached her lips and eyes.

They drank the bottle between them while they got ready, sharing the mirror, brushing past each other as they moved around the bedroom. Did they have sex in the shower first? Tom can still recall the warm squeaking of her flesh and the tang of mint and Champagne on her breath, the water streaming down her body. They had sex all the time back then. He can definitely see Sandra all svelte in that wool figure-hugging dress (there's a photo of them, so he knows that's right) sipping the fizz as she dried her hair. Her hair was long and dark in those days, with hints of deep burgundy when it caught the light.

The colour is bright yellow with golden glimmers. The bead is very fine. The aroma's top notes are subdued and sombre and dry.

The second bottle must have been three months later. The week before their wedding. Ikea flutes this time – an engagement present. They were in the kitchen looking through the RSVPs, the gift list and Tom's cost spreadsheet. They were both a little prickly, sharing second and third thoughts as doubt crept in. Tom was concerned about the mounting costs. Everything was astronomical. Wedding nerves, they both acknowledged. They discussed it all in a sedate fashion until the Champagne kicked in and Sandra screwed up his neat spreadsheets, cupped his face in her hands and told him to focus on what it was really about. 'It's just about us,' she said, 'the two of us together.' They made love on the kitchen floor. Tom remembers how he poured Champagne over Sandra's breasts and how her hair pooled out onto the tiles, and how eagerly she reached for him. They didn't know she was pregnant then.

Notes of smoked, roasted, malted scents with hints of toasted sesame seed ... as well as rather original oceanic notes, including a touch of nori seaweed.

They got through five bottles during their first Christmas. Sandra was very pregnant, and only had a couple of inches of Moët in a Bucks Fizz on Christmas morning. But Tom felt they deserved to celebrate; they had just moved in to their new house in Southwick, on the coast near Brighton. London was too expensive and not ideal for bringing up kids. They'd have been lucky to get a one bed in London. The new house had three bedrooms and was close to Sandra's parents, so they would be on hand to help. Living costs were going to escalate with a child. Tom had studied the statistics: £218,000 from birth to twenty-one.

They had friends over on Boxing Day. They drank from Dartington crystal flutes. A wedding present. Despite the drizzle they walked down to the beach after lunch. Tom stood behind Sandra, his arms stretched around the warm bulk of her stomach, his face against her neck and hair, inhaling the smell of shampoo mixed with the saline air. He felt a kick against his palm and wondered, for a moment, about chemistry, and what this vessel contained; what their random genetic mix might produce. Sandra pressed back against him as they watched the waves gather, heave and break with numbing regularity.

Subsequently come softer, warmer notes of wax, honey...

Tom took a bottle to the maternity ward the day after Freya was born. Sandra looked different. She had been claret-skinned and breathless and sweaty after the birth. Now she was soft and flushed and full-bodied. Freya was sleeping in a see-through plastic cot and Tom thought she was perfect. Her smooth skin was the colour of Champagne. Later he was told it was a touch of jaundice, but at the time she seemed tinged with gold. He felt a surge of warmth, a lurching primal element that shuddered through him. He could scale mountains, destroy armies, hurl himself in front of on-coming cars. They drank the Moët out of cups from the hospital canteen. Tom etched a heart in the polystyrene with his thumb-nail. Their three initials were captured inside.

... almond, biscuit and dried fruits (banana and coconut).

The christening. A local flint-stone church in Southwick. A summer storm had driven the seagulls inland and they were wheeling and squabbling around the spire as Tom and Sandra rushed belatedly through the gravestones. They were knackered and bickering and Freya was snivelling in her car seat. They'd had to change her twice before they'd left. Tom couldn't quite believe they were doing this – throwing an extortionate party and allowing their daughter to be daubed with holy water when they were both agnostic. In the end, Tom conceded, the day was a surprising success. Everyone was incredibly generous with gifts and wine. Their new NCT friends brought platters of charcuterie, canapés and tarty almond biscuits. Two of Tom's old uni friends were pregnant. The breeding thing seemed contagious. He topped up their Prosecco with relieved bonhomie. There was safety in numbers. They weren't alone in their hell of sleepless nights and endless bottles and nappies.

Sandra had cut her hair because it was 'easier to manage.' But that day she'd done something nice and it hung in a shiny Gamay bob. For the first time in ages Tom wanted to cup the weight of it in his hands and find the nape of her neck with his fingertips. They cracked open the Moët back at home, once Freya had finally gone to sleep. She looked like an angel, starfish hands flung out above her head. Tom inhaled her baby breath and talc and lavender. Sandra slipped an arm around his waist and whispered, 'If only we could bottle it.'

The palate is energetic, sustained by an invigorating tanginess with notes of citrus zest and citrus seeds.

At three, Freya was relentless. A ball of fizzing energy that only ceased when she was asleep. Sandra had lost the blurred softness. She was sharp and acerbic, accomplishing everything at top speed with an edge of suppressed irritation. When she announced, over another over-cooked stir-fry, that she was considering going back to work, Tom readily agreed. She was distant, edgy, and had not been herself lately. And besides, Tom had only ever wanted one child. That way they could do it properly: decent schools, decent house, decent holidays. Sandra's old company took her back, and they moved to a detached property on Shoreham Beach, one row back from the front, and large enough to accommodate the Spanish au-pair. Tom opened the Moët upstairs on their balcony, which afforded them a partial sea view. They clinked crystal flutes, talked about the parties they'd have, and whether Freya would need tuition to get her through the entrance exams to the prep school.

Middle notes are delicate with a slight graininess. Nuances of pine and iodine contribute to a crystalline, saline finish.

It was nothing serious. One night at a drunken conference. A woman from HR. They were briefly united by a shared penchant for salt-cod, old-world Chardonnay and Arctic Monkey lyrics. She was married but 'there was no intimacy anymore,' she told Tom, midway through their third bottle of Chablis. She touched his wrist, making him slop the Chardonnay onto his cuff. *No intimacy.* His stomach twisted as he rolled back his damp sleeve. It was true, he'd known it for months, maybe a couple of years; there was no intimacy anymore. It had oxidized, dried up. His eyes pricked as he felt a yearning emptiness in his gut. He took the HR woman to bed.

Tom had always believed that if anything of that ilk were to occur (not that he imagined it ever would), you should be man enough to keep mum. It would be pointless confessing. Self-indulgent. You'd only do it to gratify your own conscience. But the HR woman pursued him by text and email, then cornered him in a pub garden after work one day. He knocked over his bottle of Pinot as he tried to extract himself from the picnic bench. The sunlight was unflattering to her grey roots and her décolletage, which put Tom in mind of the crumpled balls of tracing paper Freya had thrown in the bin the night before. Freya had a lop-eared rabbit called Dougal; Tom passed the hutch every day when he came back from work. His dreams dilated into nightmares about Dougal's demise in a bubbling pan, and he found himself crying and confessing in Sandra's arms. 'It meant nothing,' he said, 'I'm sorry.' He resisted using the 'no intimacy' phrase, afraid of what it might uncork.

He made an effort on their anniversary and took her out for a surprise dinner at a Michelin-starred restaurant that she'd mentioned. The conversation didn't flow. When he gave the usual 10% tip she silently opened her soft green clutch bag and handed the waiter an extra tenner. Another night he cooked supper for the two of them and opened a bottle of the Moët. Mid-week. He served it in Sandra's Babycham glasses. It tasted like a different wine; slightly grainy and with the saltiness of tears. Age, they both agreed, had not improved it.

Phylloxera Epidemic. Many growers resorted to their own methods in an attempt to resolve the issue. Chemicals and pesticides were used to no avail. In desperation, some growers positioned toads under each vine, and others allowed their poultry to roam free in the hope they would eat the insects. None of these methods were successful.

Tom should never have told her but he tried not to dwell on it; hindsight was a crap drug. He persisted for a while with flowers, chocolates, and even a weekend away on a company jolly, but there was never a full recovery. At fourteen, Sandra allowed Freya to become a weekly boarder. Tom put up an initial resistance – the fees were astronomical – but he eventually acquiesced. Sandra had a promotion and a pixie haircut dyed a startling New World Chardonnay. She worked late most evenings and slept in Freya's room, so as not to disturb Tom. He wondered if she was having an affair but couldn't bring himself to ask. He prayed that her working-class morality would prevent a revenge shag.

Then, last year she was offered another promotion. The hours were longer and the commute was exhausting. Freya was on a gap year and so Sandra rented a flat in Hendon. After the first weekend she didn't come back.

Moët & Chandon 1988 Vintage Champagne, the 59th in the House's history, is a dark, precise, streamlined Champagne. This rare vintage Champagne was created in a particularly difficult harvest year.

Tom looks at the kitchen clock. She'll be here soon. He takes out the Dartington flutes. There is something reassuring about their weight and solidity. The wedding guest who bought them twenty years ago, had the foresight to opt for a classic design, and he's grateful for that. A few have broken over the years, but he was swift to replace them and even bought extras in the January sales.

When he's fishing around at the back of the cupboard for a suitable vessel for the olives, he finds one of Sandra's old Babycham glasses. He places it on the island, next to the Dartingtons. The gold rim has worn off in places and the bambi has lost its ears, but it's still looking vaguely sprightly. It spikes a memory of the first time they tasted the Moët. He has to sit down for a moment, gripping the island. If only there was a pair left. He considers serving Sandra's in the Babycham glass and his in the flute, but fears Sandra might see this as a metaphor for the chasm that yawns between them.

She rings the bell like a guest and stands awkwardly in the kitchen, looking around and fiddling with her hair.

'Sit down,' he says and pulls out her chair, but this feels wrong, as if he's giving her permission when it's still her house.

He takes the Moët from the fridge – 'Ta Dah!' – and grabs a tea towel and twists the cork before she can say no, which she will, he can tell. She hasn't sat down or taken off her coat. It is a new suede coat that makes her seem like a stranger. He wrenches off the cork, and there is the slightest pop, like a tired exhalation.

'Come on, let's try it. Pointless saving it. It'll probably be off. But we can try, can't we? Let's give it a go. See what we think.'

Sandra shrugs, takes off her coat and lays it with neat precision across the back of the chair. 'Okay. I've got twenty minutes.'

Tom's heart contracts and expands as he looks at her. She's gained a little weight. In a good way. He suddenly sees Freya, in her cheek bones and the shape of her mouth. For a moment he is afraid he might cry.

He sniffs the bottle. 'What do you think? It still smells like Champagne, but concentrated. Almost like Tequila?' It is like pouring honey. They clink flutes, and drink. There are echoes of the original flavours, but it is flat and slightly bitter. Tom gets out the olives, pimento stuffed, Sandra's favourite. 'This might help.' He offers the bowl. 'And we haven't let it breathe. It probably needs a bit of time. A rest.' He tops them both up. They sip the Champagne and talk about Freya's latest adventure, grape picking in Bordeaux.

Sandra picks up her clutch bag. 'Remember when you bought this?'

'Of course. For our engagement party. A surprise. You'd gone off looking for more Babycham glasses.'

She nods, takes another sip of Champagne. 'I watched you buy it. You haggled for an eternity.'

'Really? You sure?'

'Yes. Quite sure.'

Sandra belts up her coat, then pulls out her hair from

beneath the collar. It fans onto her shoulders in a wash of deep Bordeaux.

'Your hair's grown. It looks lovely.'

'Well. Hair does that. Thanks, Tom.'

'You could stay.'

'I'm staying at friends. A dinner party.'

'How about next weekend?'

She stares at him.

'Only there's one bottle left.'

'No. That's the last one.'

Tom shakes his head. 'There's another one. Stored better. Why don't you come down. We can see if it's lasted. I'll open it earlier. Prepare it. Let it breathe. We could give it a try.'

She shrugs. 'I don't know. Maybe. Let me check. I'll phone you.'

When she's gone, Tom tidies up the kitchen. He cling-films the last couple of olives and finishes the Champagne; it seems a waste to leave it.

He clicks on his Google history. The Moët is still there. £330. That doesn't include delivery.

Tom hesitates, his stomach clenching, his cursor hovering over the 'buy' button.

Beaujolais Day
by Kate North

Nick and Debbie were at *Le Monde Farci* for a three-course meal and a carafe of Beaujolais Nouveau. The restaurant was extremely busy and they were glad they'd booked. They'd been given complimentary glasses of Champagne when they arrived, and a waiter apologised in advance for any delay that might occur as they were short-staffed.

Nick and Debbie didn't mind so much as they had plenty to catch up on. Debbie had just come out of a relationship with a short, angry man called Jude. They had been together for about a year, having met at a friend's wedding. Debbie put an end to it when, for the third time, he lost his shit after drinking a bottle of vodka. He wrecked the living-room door in an argument, accusing Debbie of not listening properly to what he was saying. He left that night and the following morning Debbie packed up all the remaining Jude-related items in her house. She placed them in a bag and then put the bag inside the storage box in her front garden – a box she usually used for her organic veg delivery. She sent him a text asking him to collect it while she was at work. Nick admired her clarity.

'Three strikes and out,' said Debbie.

'No further discussion required,' agreed Nick.

When a flustered waiter eventually came to their table, they both ordered chicken liver parfait to start. For mains, Nick ordered a bavette steak and Debbie a roasted poussin. When he asked for the carafe of Beaujolais, the waiter's eyes met Nick's briefly before looking down at his note pad. The waiter apologised: 'I am so sorry, sir, we have a slight problem with the Beaujolais tonight.'

'What?' said Nick. He looked at the waiter; there was

something familiar about him. It was his eyes, or the shape of his head or something. He had a thick neck and round nose like a small tomato. Nick was sure he knew him.

'There's been a mix up with our supplier and we don't have any Beaujolais, I'm afraid.'

'No Beaujolais?' Debbie's nose crinkled with incredulity, 'On Beaujolais Day?'

'That's correct,' said the waiter, 'we are terribly sorry.'

'But we came here for the special Beaujolais menu,' said Nick.

The waiter looked towards Debbie while replying to Nick: 'May I offer you our 2011 Pinot Noir from Burgundy, at half price by way of an apology? It is the nearest thing we have to the Beaujolais.' The waiter twiddled his pen awkwardly. His nails were chewed to the quick.

They accepted the alternative wine. While the waiter leaned over to take their menus, Nick experienced a pang of recognition. The waiter's small tomato nose. It shocked him so deeply he dug his nails into his thighs and gave a shallow gasp. Debbie didn't notice his gasp and carried on talking about The Nightmare That Was Jude.

'I won't miss his weird ironing obsession.' Debbie widened her eyes. 'He even ironed his socks. It's the sign of a sociopath.'

The waiter was Mark Stevens. He was a pupil at St. Asaph's and he'd made Nick's life hell for a year. The only class they had together was PE, but it was enough. The bullying was relentless, public and cruel.

The bullying had started in the showers, but over the course of year nine it had moved into break times as well. 'Here comes the faggot,' Mark would yell, the minute Nick got in the showers. The PE teacher would ignore it, and Mark's gang would shove and push until Nick fell on the wet tiles. At lunch-time, they would follow him around the yard repeating, '*Faggot, faggot, faggot.*' Sometimes one of the gang would shoulder barge into him, or tug at the hair on the back of his head. One time, after PE, it reached a climax. Nick rushed to the shower first in an effort to finish before the bullies arrived. He had just rinsed the soap from himself and was reaching for his towel when Mark appeared and whipped it away from him.

'Gimme my towel,' stammered Nick.

'Gimme my towel,' mimicked Mark in a girly voice.

Nick made a lunge for the towel and Mark held it high above him. He was significantly taller than Nick.

'Give it back!' Nick shouted.

The boys in the class gathered and Mark smiled at his audience, then glared at Nick, 'Or what?'

Mark kicked Nick in the groin and a deep and dizzying pain erupted between his legs. He began to shake. '*Fight, fight, fight,*' the class chanted. Mark loomed in front, gesturing for Nick to hit him back. Nick sobbed and buckled forward. Some boys laughed while others continued chanting. Then the boys hushed. A momentary stasis was followed by a strange cry that emerged from deep within Mark. Nick had never heard anything like it. It was like a wolf or some horrid bird.

When their mains came, Nick and Debbie had almost finished the bottle of Pinot Noir. A different waiter had brought it to them along with their starters, and Mark continued his shift on another table. Nick could see him taking orders from a large family near the bar area.

He cut into his bavette and watched the pink meat flake apart. Debbie poured the rest of the bottle.

After the fight Nick woke in the hospital with a fractured

skull. He learned that Mark had been expelled to the crappy comp on the other side of town. Apparently, the teachers had to pull Mark off Nick. When Nick came back to school the teachers made a point of smiling at him, which was nice at first but then it felt somewhat creepy.

'Should we order another?' asked Debbie, tapping the empty bottle.

'Why not?' said Nick. His steak was perfectly delicate and he was having a good time catching up with Debbie. On top of it all, Mark Stevens had turned out to be a waiter at the age of thirty-nine, while Nick had a senior management role in Lloyds and lived in a listed building with an Aga. This definitely deserved a second bottle of wine.

Nick had only moved a couple of months ago, to an old chapel on the edge of the Brecon Beacons. All major renovations were complete and now he was working on the furniture and décor. Debbie asked how it was going and he showed her pictures on his phone of his polished floors, his cleaned masonry façade and the aged beams in the lounge. Debbie cooed and asked whether there would be a house party. 'Maybe,' said Nick, but he wanted to get all the furnishings sorted in the first instance. Currently he was sleeping with a sheet for a curtain over his bedroom window. His view took in Fan Fawr and the reservoir, and it felt as if he was uncovering a painting at a gallery opening when he pulled the sheet back each morning.

Sometimes he stood for a good five minutes contemplating the view. The light was never the same. On clear days it shone over the water, making it look like an oil slick. Other times it speared the clouds. It was better than a work-out at the gym or a shot of coffee. It made him feel alive. He showed Debbie a picture of his view: 'It's like heaven, but beyond,' she gushed.

Their new waiter came back and they discussed the distinct merits of a cheese board and a soufflé, then went for one of each. Debbie poured more wine. Nick excused himself and stood up. He had to steady himself for a moment and Debbie giggled.

'You're a bad influence!' Nick declared. He walked slowly across the restaurant to the door marked 'Messieurs' with a little picture of a moustache underneath.

Nick supported himself at the sink. After washing his hands he wiped the back of his neck with cool water. He felt less drunk in here than in the bustle of the dimly-lit restaurant. A stall door creaked behind him and Mark walked out of the cubicle. Nick tensed as they made eye contact via the mirror above the sink. Mark's skin was sallow and appeared yellow under the light. Nick considered his range of options. Even though he was very drunk he felt a certain clarity. He smiled at Mark, who responded with a smile in return. Nick turned to face him and Mark stepped back, walking into the stall door as he did so. He opened his mouth to say something but his bottom lip hung, creating a silent 'o'.

Nick placed his hand on Mark's shoulder and gave it a squeeze. A really hard squeeze: he could feel Mark's muscle between his thumb and forefinger. Mark winced and a tear dropped from his right eye. Nick's hand turned numb with effort. He gave one last extra-hard squeeze before releasing his grip. Then he regarded Mark fully, up and down.

Back at the table Nick shared his cheeseboard with Debbie, who gave him half of her soufflé in return. They talked about when it would be good to meet again and which restaurant they might try. There was a new Turkish place Debbie had heard was authentic. Nick insisted on paying the bill and Debbie said she would pay next time.

They flagged a taxi outside the castle and Debbie was

slumped against Nick's shoulder as they pulled into her drive.

'It's been a lovely evening, darling.'

Nick agreed and they got out of the taxi. They wobbled to her front door and laughed as she struggled to get her key into the lock. She missed several times and they ended up having to put the key in the lock together, Nick's hand over Debbie's. A blood blister, the size of a grain of rice, had formed under his thumbnail.

'It was a lovely night,' said Nick, 'and not a drop of Beaujolais passed my lips.'

Sweden

by Karen Stevens

'So,' says Mike, studying Issie closely, after the third bottle of wine is almost finished, 'you're our new neighbour.'

Issie feels the heat of Mike's expansive smile slipping over her.

'Oh dear,' Mandy gives Mike's knee a stern pat. 'Issie looks truly worried.'

'Why?' Mike asks, amused.

'It's the *fourth* time you've mentioned it this evening, Mike.'

'Well, she *is* our new neighbour!' Mike raises his glass to Issie, as if to say, *So cheers to that.*

'Issie *and* Chris are our new neighbours,' Mandy reminds Mike, voice clipped.

Issie's drunk too much and way too fast to keep up with Mike and Mandy. They are seated opposite on her salmon-pink sofa, looking surprisingly sober. Mike wears a white Ralph Lauren shirt and Mandy wears a pale silk blouse tucked neatly into the waistband of her dark jeans. What possessed Issie to invite them round for a drink? Her son, Josh, has been gone for a week now and their new home is too quiet, but Chris was right – this whole idea's bizarre. Middle class.

Chris enters the living room with another bottle of Sauvignon Blanc and a bottle of Shiraz. He's wearing his ancient Rolling Stones T-shirt. 'There's just the rough stuff after this, Mandy,' he announces with a rueful smile.

'We don't mind. We've had our fair share of grog,' she replies, with a flick of her hand.

'Surely, you're a vintage wine and Champagne drinker,' Chris says, and Mandy gives a stilted laugh, unsure if it's a compliment.

Chris places the bottles on the glass-topped side table and begins organising more drinks with almost childish concentration. Issie watches Mandy assessing Chris's loose, big-lipped mouth. *Odd-looking*, she can see Mandy thinking. Issie finds Chris's mouth both odd and appealing, depending on her mood.

'It feels like you've been here for months, not weeks, Issie.' Mandy nods at Issie's bright Ikea rug and Josh's train track in its centre. 'I must say, when the house was put up for rent, we were a little concerned about who was going to move in.'

'Ooh, I'd stop there, Mandy,' Chris warns, though his voice is light, almost teasing, as he hands back Mandy's glass, refilled. 'Issie's a Housing Options Officer for the City Council.'

Mike's eyes brighten, interested. He takes his glass from Chris. His forearm is solid and furred, not unlike Josh's father's, Issie thinks, briefly unsettled by the similarity.

'You could say we work in the same area, Issie,' Mike says. 'I'm an architect.'

'You build affordable housing?' Issie asks.

'Well. No. Private projects.'

'So you don't work in the same area at all,' Chris points out.

Issie feels bad for Mike when he averts his eyes from Chris's self-satisfied smile. 'There's a crisis. The country needs all types of housing,' she says, trying to make amends.

'That's not what you said this morning.'

Issie frowns at Chris for stirring it; for bringing politics into what's meant to be a social evening. 'Anyway, Mandy, we probably *aren't* the best neighbours. Josh is a typical two year old. He can be pretty noisy.'

Mike and Mandy exchange glances.

'He's at that – that really boisterous age.'

'Where is Josh – in bed?' Mandy asks. Her eyes roam over the living room, as if she expects to find him.

'He's – on holiday with his father.'

'Oh. I thought he must be here.' Mandy nods at Josh's Brio 'Little Forest Starter Set.'

It was Chris's idea to buy Josh a housewarming present to help him settle into his new home. He ran around the living room when Chris presented it gift-wrapped in silver paper, then hunkered down to work, clumsily putting the circular wooden track together. He attached the carriage with its load of logs to the magnetic rear of the black train engine, then spent hours shunting it around the track, making high-pitched train noises and crash sounds.

'Issie can't bring herself to take it down,' Chris says, passing Issie her wine. His eyes are glazed.

'He spent so long building it,' Issie explains, and Mandy smiles, as if she understands perfectly.

Chris slumps on the sofa next to Issie, his long legs splayed out. 'Yeah,' he says, stretching the word out lazily. 'He's with his dad, staying at his grandparents' in Sweden, for two weeks.'

'Sweden?' Mandy's finely-pencilled eyebrows rise. 'He must be having a lovely time.'

'Bound to be,' Chris says, as if that's an end to it.

Issie looks into her wine glass, through the pale Sauvignon Blanc. She imagines flying like a bird over the brackish Baltic Sea to Sweden; to where her son, tiny, stands on the edge of a pebbled shore grabbing at his father's hand.

How can a mother let her child be so far away? she knows Mandy will ask Mike later. She must seem like a hippy to them in her loose maxi dress and wrist and ankle bracelets. She's braless and barefooted, without a lick of varnish on her toe nails. She takes her mobile from her dress pocket to check for a message. Maybe Josh has sent her one of his little texts via his father: *I caught a crab today. I had ice-cream for tea.*

There's nothing.

'I imagine Josh's bedroom is the back room,' Mandy says.

'That's right.'

'Well – just beware of that window when he's home. The windowsill's only a foot from the floor and it's so easy for a little one to stand on it and lean out and – well – doesn't bear thinking about. I was always pulling down the sash when I babysat for Suzy.'

'You used to babysit here?' Issie asks. Her head reels, though she's unsure if it's the wine.

'I know this house inside out.'

Mandy gives Issie a knowing nod, as if re-claiming something she once owned, and Issie's stomach tightens.

'I'd get the agency to fix a lock to Josh's bedroom window,' Mandy says. 'And I'd get the drains checked out. Sometimes an appalling whiff comes from under the kitchen sink.'

Issie studies Mandy's short brown bob and decides it doesn't suit her, just emphasises her roundness, the jowls that will flop from under her chin in a few more years.

'That's a nice-looking instrument,' Mike says, nodding at Chris's guitar propped up in the far corner. 'Is it a Gibson?'

Chris pushes himself up in his seat. 'Yeah. I picked one up a few weeks ago after months of flirting.'

'Play something,' Mandy says.

'Maybe later. When I'm *really* pissed.'

'Oh no don't, Chris.' Issie doesn't want the neighbours to think they'll be too noisy. They are perfectly suitable for living in this neat street.

'Can I have a look?' Mike asks, nodding at the guitar.

'Sure.'

When Mike gets up, his broad body seems to fill the living room.

'The Gibson has a sweeter tone than a Fender.' Mike's hand glides over its curves appreciatively. 'It's definitely the best guitar out there right now.'

'You play?' Issie asks, surprised.

'No!' Mandy laughs. 'Mike was going to learn last year and spent endless weeks researching guitars on the internet – and that's as far as it's got.' Her smile drops when she sees Mike's mottled cheeks.

'So what have you settled on?' Chris asks.

'Well –' Mike returns to the sofa. 'I rather like –' He loosens a button on his shirt, revealing a greying tuft of hair, 'I rather like the Gibson J15.'

'Nice one.'

Mike relaxes back, relieved, and Mandy gives his hand a squeeze.

'I still do a fair bit of research before buying,' Chris says. 'I bought her for under a thousand pounds.'

'*Her.* Sounds like you have some competition, Issie.' Mandy eyes Issie over the rim of her glass, then swigs her drink.

'Nothing compares to holding a Gibson. Not even a woman,' Chris says, and laughs when Issie rolls her eyes. 'When I take her in my arms it feels like she was made just for me.'

'Surely *nothing* in life compares to holding a woman.' Mike places his square hand on Mandy's thigh and winks at Issie.

Was it a wink? Issie's seeing double now and closes one eye to bring Mike into sharper focus. He has dark penetrating eyes and closely cropped hair to disguise his advancing baldness – and though he could shift a few pounds he is a handsome man.

Mike and Chris are talking about garages. The conversation has covered Ska music, favourite films, allotments. All the good wine has now been drunk, and the third bottle of cheap plonk is almost done. Beneath the light chat and shared interests, Issie can detect competitiveness between the two men.

'It's warm in here, isn't it?' Mandy puffs the neck of her silk blouse in and out.

Issie's been putting off opening the patio doors. When she stands the neighbours will see she's smashed. She gets up and the room swirls, but she manages to right herself and walk.

'Pissed again,' Chris slurs, as she fumbles with the French doors.

'Tricky lock, actually,' Mandy tells him. 'Pull the door inwards, Issie, and *then* turn the key anti-clockwise.'

Fuck off, Issie thinks, attempting to do as instructed.

'Here. Let me help.'

She hadn't heard Mike get up. His hand covers her own and he guides her until the key finally turns. Something transfers between them, an electric warmth.

'Tricky lock,' he says briskly, stepping back.

'See – I told you so,' Mandy says, delighted.

The garden is small with just a few scrubby bushes and a rectangle of lawn that has a bald square in its centre. The owners must have had a playhouse there. Issie almost trips, inwardly cursing her pathetic ability to hold drink. She can still feel the light pressure of Mike's fingers on her own and gulps back the air as if it is water. She shambles around the perimeter of the garden, irritated by Mandy's claim on *her* home. *Get the drains checked out; pull the door inwards; fix a lock to Josh's bedroom window.*

I was crying about you, Josh told her over the phone this morning. She'd sneaked downstairs early while Chris was still asleep and dialled the number, alert for any movement from above. *I was missing you*, Josh said. For a second she thought he was going to cry, could hear the waver in his chubby voice. But then he was telling her about a present he'd bought for her and his voice was excited and fast. *A star*, he'd said, and he was shouting out to the others, *I telled her, I telled my mummy.* There was a sudden clatter and the sound of Josh's feet running off, then Josh's father informing her coldly that Josh had bought her a star-shaped cushion.

Josh's truck lies on the grass on its side, from when he'd abandoned it for a biscuit. Issie takes its plastic handle and stands it back on its squat red wheels, then wishes she hadn't bothered. It looks so sad and alone in its upright position, as if waiting for Josh to clamber aboard.

She takes out her mobile and punches in her code, then punches again until she manages to get the right numbers. Josh's face fills the screen and Issie almost gasps at his beaming smile, his blondness. *Mummy misses you*, she texts to his father's phone.

Issie absorbs the numbed atmosphere as she returns to sit by Chris on the sofa. His arms are flopped on his lap, his jaw slack. She nudges him once, twice. His heavy-lidded eyes open and roll upwards – *Thank fuck you're back*. Mike is resting into the opposite sofa, wine glass loosely clutched in his hand. His thighs and biceps are dark hills in the dusky light. In comparison, Mandy seems shrunken. Her eyes are glistening circles staring fixedly at Josh's train track. *Keep your eyes off*, Issie wants to tell her.

'Chris!' Issie digs her elbow into his ribs.

'Yup,' he barks, 'Yup.'

'Play something for us.' Issie must rouse them all, like a proper host. 'Play something,' she insists.

Chris's eyes open. He stares ahead, then shakes his head to make sense of where he is. He struggles up and switches off the Paolo Nutini that's been playing, takes his guitar and stands in the centre of the room, legs splayed. It's like cold water has been flicked at Mike and Mandy; they look startlingly alert.

'This is for you, my *señorita*,' he announces to Issie.

'Oh don't, Chris,' Issie begs, though her eyes tell him different.

He strums a light Spanish-sounding riff and Mandy attempts a clap. He watches Issie – lips pouting, face brooding – and Issie swigs her wine to suppress drunken giggles.

'*Siempre siempre tu coño … Siempre siempre tu culo …*' Half singing, half laughing when he says the word *coño* and *culo*, black eyes locked on Issie's – '*illuminando mi cara …*' His voice is rich and sensual with wine – '*como un sol grande …*' he finishes, voice dipping dramatically along with a flourish of Spanish-style strumming that Mike – pofaced – does not appear to appreciate.

Issie and Chris giggle helplessly and Mike and Mandy watch, sloshed and bemused. Issie loves the secret knowledge that rushes between her and Chris: fast, intravenous. When he'd chatted up Issie on a hen night after his gig in The Richmond Arms, she told him she'd lived in Spain in her early twenties and he made her repeat every profanity she'd learned in Spanish until he could say it back to her word-perfect: *culo-culo-culo-coño-coño-coño*.

She'd loved his ridiculous accent and mischievous eyes, the way he'd made her laugh out loud. On the first afternoon of moving in together he'd sung his love song to her, this ridiculous love song – *Siempre siempre tu coño …*

Always, always your cunt … Always, always your arse … illuminating my face … like a big sun …

'If a building is to stand the test of time it needs symmetry,'

Mike slurs, and attempts to sit upright. 'I realise you were having some fun just then, Chris – but I'm sure you'll agree it's the same with music. Good music requires symmetry.'

Chris places his guitar back in its corner. 'There has to be harmony, Mike,' he says, as if Mike's set a challenge. 'Some sort of regularity, I guess. But it's important to break the expectation from time to time, to prevent boredom, don't you think?'

'Hear-hear!' Issie giggles.

Mike's attention shifts to appraise Issie, and heat spreads across her throat.

'Any more wine?' Mandy shakes her empty glass in front of her flushed face.

Chris picks up a bottle and lopes across the living room, his thin legs invisible under his baggy jeans. Chris's legs remind Issie of a coyote's: bony and sinewy, oddly muscled. The thought – the distraction – is a relief. 'Careful!' she warns, when he almost treads on Josh's train track.

'Yesss, careful,' Mandy manages.

Who does Mandy think she is – warning Chris about Josh's train track? Issie looks at Mike to see if he, too, is irritated by Mandy's need to take over. He is still watching her, and she feels a sudden surge of superiority under his bullish intensity. She shifts her back so that her braless breasts press against her dress.

Mandy shuffles to the edge of the sofa and half-drops her wine glass onto the teak side table. The room is moving in and out of focus, yet Issie must be vigilant. A mother is always vigilant. The rental agency's representative, all marching and jackbooted, will arrive in two weeks' time to inspect the premises, clutching a clipboard.

Mike and Mandy – Issie's sure – have never rented a home; never experienced the humiliation of being financially checked out, of being informed in a tiny high-street office that they must not stain the carpets or walls, that they are not allowed to smoke or have pets or choose where to hang their pictures.

'I'm still a home owner,' Issie says, as if she's been accused of something.

'Yeah,' Chris sneers, topping up Mandy's glass. 'The bastard refuses to leave the house. *That's* why we're renting this overpriced box.'

'These houses are hardly boxes,' Mike bristles. 'Both bedrooms are good doubles.'

Issie thinks of the parties she and Josh's father used to throw; her friends drinking wine and chatting comfortably around her kitchen island. Good friends. Established friends. Everything safe and familiar.

'We're paying £1200 for a two-bedroom box, Mandy.' Chris plonks the wine bottle on the glass-topped side table.

'But you're paying for the neighbourhood.' Mandy's voice is slow, drenched with wine. 'The lovely school.'

'It's a good school.' Issie nods and feels sick.

Chris lies flat out on the carpet and releases a snort of boredom.

'We don't have children, do we, Mike?' Mandy tips her head sideways to look at him. 'But it's a good school, I think.'

Her face is loose and drunk, *a little desperate*, Issie thinks.

'Time to go.' Mike taps his chunky watch face impatiently.

Later, when Issie accuses Chris of stirring it; of spending the evening making digs about 'housing' just to push the neighbours into leaving, he'll say – *Josh is away. This is our time, Issie. What the fuck was that all about, anyway?* Pissed. Belligerent. She will be defensive – she can see it now – accusing him of being classist when she knows he's right.

Next week they will pass Mark and Mandy in the High Street and pretend not to have seen each other.

Issie glares at Chris, sprawled like a ten year-old on the carpet, always vying with Josh for her attention, even when he isn't here. *This is our time*, he keeps telling her. Yesterday, she had to sneak out to the shed to use her mobile. *They're still asleep*, Josh's grandma told her. Issie watched the house through the dusty shed window, ready to hang up if Chris emerged into the garden to find her. *You want to call back later?* Issie didn't know what to say, just, *Is he okay?* The grandmother said he was fine, that cool tone melting, just a little. *Fine*, she'd said. *He still enjoys feeding the chickens, throwing stones in the sea. Same as when you were – well, little changes here.*

Issie feels herself dividing from Chris, sucking backwards into herself like the sea. And what *is* this all about? she keeps asking herself, ever since they moved in. Her eyes dart around the room, absorbing it in sharp fragments. The carpet and sofas are unknown flat planes, the people as strange as apes. Soon enough, Josh will not remember Chris or this house, and she will barely recall this awful pissed evening … So much of her life will now be like this – moments that pass her by and move off into the distance.

She squints at her mobile. No messages. *Mummy misses you.* Why hasn't Josh answered? *It's late*, she chides herself. It's eleven o'clock here and midnight in Sweden. Issie imagines her son and his father – still her husband – curled together in the darkness of their Swedish bedroom; their light puffs of breath, the twitch of Josh's hand.

'I miss Josh,' she thinks she hears herself say. Perhaps she didn't say it.

Chris sighs.

She must have said it.

'You're half asleep, Mandy. Time to go,' Mike orders,

struggling up from the sofa.

'For God's sake, Issie – it's way too late. Don't embarrass yourself,' Chris warns, as her hands fumble with the mobile.

Josh's face jumps out from the screen's blackness.

'They're on holiday. Stop harassing them, for fuck's sake!'

'It's *my* right; *I'm* his mother.'

'We're off now,' Mike calls from the doorway.

Issie looks to Mandy for support. She's slumped back on the sofa, her eyes glassy and fluttering into sleep. Issie searches her contacts for Josh's grandmother's number, but the process is too hard – her fingers won't work properly.

'Give me the mobile, Issie. Give it here!' Chris's long legs slip against the smooth surface of the carpet as he attempts to rise. His foot kicks out, dismantling Josh's train track.

Issie hears the wooden clatter and lunges off the sofa with a horrified squeal.

'Oh dear.' Mandy's eyes open in alarm.

Issie hunches over the train set to protect it before Chris can inflict any more damage. The track is broken into individual pieces, the magnetic engine severed from its carriages. A wounded sound escapes from her throat.

'Come on now,' Mike is saying. His hands scoop under Issie's armpits. 'Come and get a glass of water.'

White walls sweep past Issie as Mike helps her out. In the kitchen, he rests his hands on her shoulders.

'Josh built that train track,' she says tearfully. '*He* broke it on purpose.'

'It's just the booze, Issie.' Mike sways. 'Try and calm yourself.'

The high row of cupboards behind Mike is dark and unfamiliar, Mike a broad and muscled shape.

And what was it all about? The boozing. This *recklessness*.

Why did she give away so much?

'Don't dwell on it,' Mike whispers, as if she's spoken. 'Sometimes, it's wise not to think too much.'

His hands run downwards over her loose cotton dress towards her buttocks. Instinctively, she arches her back. Through the tiny square of kitchen window, she watches the stars and imagines they are sliding through the darkness towards Sweden.

Bones

by Hannah Stevens

He noticed how she touched the barmaid's hand when she paid for her drink. Already he understood. It was in the way she breathed too: as if an ache stopped the muscles from expanding like they should. Tonight his loneliness made him brave. He touched her arm.

'I'm Henry,' he said. 'Can I buy you a drink?'

Later, Bethan suggested a hotel.

'It would be sad to say goodbye so early,' she said. 'Aren't we having a good time?'

This had never happened to him before. He wasn't that kind of man. Except tonight there was no reason to say no, and so he nodded his head, followed her.

'Do you have a room high up?' she asked the reception staff as they booked in, 'one where we can see the whole of the sky?'

The boy behind the counter paused, checked his screen. 'No problem,' he said, and he gave them the key.

The hotel room is blue. It reminds Henry of hospital visits. Maybe this isn't a good idea, but it feels too late to say no. He can hear something buzzing now the door is closed and he looks over to the window. A wasp crawls across the glass. Bethan opens the sash and they watch it fly away.

Her skin is cold at first but soon there is heat beneath his fingertips. She's taken off her clothes and he thinks that she's lovely, although a little thin. He can feel her ribs and he shakes now that he holds her. He can't decide whether he should hold her more tightly or touch her more lightly.

The bed sinks beneath them and the springs press into his back.

Henry runs his fingertips along her spine and then holds her hips. They are sharp in his hands and he'd forgotten how this feels.

Afterwards, when they smoke together, she opens the window wider, pushes the sash upwards, as high as it will go. There should probably be a safety catch but there's nothing, and he thinks it opens too far.

They've been drinking for hours now. She pours them the last of the wine and Henry realises it's light outside. He hears cars, and birds beginning to sing. She's talking quickly, and he can't decide exactly why but he thinks that she looks different to yesterday.

She swallows the last of her drink and he looks at the empty bottles across the room. It takes him a minute to realise what she's saying, even though she's talking slowly and the words are simple and neat in her mouth. She tells him about the time she laid down one night in the freezing cold. She'd taken off her clothes and there'd been a frost. It was in a park not far from where she used to live, a few months after her baby died.

'Can you believe I woke up the next day?' she asks. 'It was as if nothing had happened.' Henry doesn't answer because he doesn't know what to say. There are two rolled up notes beside her. The white powder has gone now and he's glad. She tells him about her husband who destroyed her with other women, and then she sits on the sill and points to her face.

'He used to tell me how beautiful this was,' she says. 'Not anymore.'

He wants to touch her again but she seems so far away. This is the story of his life: if only he was brave enough to stand up and move towards her. He notices a rash on her throat: a flush of red across the pale skin. The sky is silver and flat and the smoke she blows from her mouth rushes through the open window.

'My baby was called Gabriel,' she says. 'But now he's dead.' She throws the cigarette from the window and lights another with a match made of black wood. She'd picked the matches up from the bar as they left. He'd noticed her nails and the white half-moons in them as she closed her palm around the box. He imagines that her hands feel cold now because it is cold outside. He thinks of her wet mouth less than an hour before; remembers how it was warm.

She's quiet then, moves her hand to just below her nose, holds it there. When she takes it away, Henry sees there's blood on her face.

'This runs in the family,' she says, 'my daughter gets nose-bleeds too.' And she laughs, but he doesn't get the joke. He understands that things are beginning to swerve out of control and he doesn't know what he should do. This morning he's less brave and more sober. He hesitates, hands her a tissue. He watches the clock on the wall as he waits for the bleeding to stop. He tells her how he's sorry for everything; sorry for it all, and if only things could be different.

He hears the traffic outside but the room is silent.

Bethan leans out of the sash window, looks at the sky, looks down.

'Do you know that birds have hollow bones so they can fly?' she says. Henry shakes his head. He's never thought of this before.

Bethan leans out further and further again. There's a blur of flesh and a rush of air. Henry stands and reaches out for her, but she has already gone and there is nothing for him to hold.

I Know Where I'm Going

by Jane Feaver

Though they'd come this way by daylight, it was a different proposition in the dark. At this distance, all that distinguished the cottage was the lozenge of light in the storm porch, and, to the left, the small carpark, long deserted, its board of regulations like a ghostly flag. When she turned away there was no light at all. This was a test of her mettle; it would show him the extent to which she'd made the place her own. There was a briny stench, a sponginess to the air. If she aimed straight out she'd hit the dunes; keep going, and sooner or later she'd arrive at the sea. Then what? She was hopeful that he'd follow her out. This would be the story: he'd bide his time – long enough to give her a fright – but then appear from the gloom like a piece of the landscape broken off.

There were no stars; a sea fret ballooned towards her. As the tarmac gave out, her footsteps made a muffled sound like slippers. The ground crumbled where she trod. She remembered the pot-holes: you could twist an ankle if you weren't careful. Banks of sand loomed ahead of her. She shuffled more cautiously, determined not to go back, not yet. The air scooted round, hissing in her ears. It tasted of the langoustines they'd picked up from a doorstep on the road out of Kilchoan, that first day, when everything was heaven. He'd brought her here, to this undulating stretch of sand and marram grass, pronouncing the word for her, *machair*, and they'd watched the sun dissolve into the sea, gilding the water, the sand. *Machair*: it was a different word again in the dark, dense and furry as a jumper.

She was groggy from three nights of drinking more than she should. Her breath was shallow and came in little puffs.

He will find me, she said to herself, believing it. He'd come and fetch her and bring her home, and they'd sit together watching the fire burn out, easy and companionable as two old dogs.

She veered to the left, fumbling towards what looked like a gulley in the dunes. Earlier they'd found a sheep upturned in the receding tide, its legs like furniture, drowned in its own fleece. Her heart was banging. It was more like climbing than walking. She climbed until the near horizon dropped away and the buzz of ocean was suddenly upon her. She spilled down the bank of sand, ankle deep, blownopen by a wind that shot straight in off the sea. Her hair whipped her face. There was no sign of him, of anyone. Her brain whirred. *All is not lost. It is only a test.* He'd come and find her so that the night could disarm them both and knock their heads together.

He'd been two years ahead of her at Oxford, but had seemed much older, man-sized and swarthy in his secondhand suit. He could have been straight out of an Italian film, but his accent was from Glasgow, a low, seductive drawl, full of gravel and honey. Most nights he could be found holding court in the pool room of the Royal Oak. What was she reading? he'd ask, sitting out a game to suggest new words, books that she should read. *The fury of men's gullets, and their groins*: where's that from? – every cell in her body, fired and jumping.

The cottage belonged to his mother. Sanna, the place was called, and in his mouth it had sounded like a bell, a call to prayer.

I Know Where I'm Going was her favourite film, she must have told him: the girl who takes the train up to the Scottish islands but is diverted by a whirlpool and a laird.

The girl he took home would be the girl he'd marry, he

said, licking his Rizla paper and eyeing her as if to say, *no chance!*

There'd been a moment, a drunken evening in her final year. He'd been abroad, and had turned up out of the blue, visiting old haunts, he'd said. In her room in the attic of the shared house they'd stripped themselves of clothes – practically, no fuss – and she'd climbed into her narrow bed, pressed to the wall, too beside herself to sleep, his naked back looming before her like a whale's, pores breathing sweetly of hops and heat. She hardly dared touch him, not with her hands. In the morning she could smell the rankness of her nerves, worrying that if she moved he'd smell them too, lying awake until the rest of the house dispersed, and he could make his getaway.

Much later, when she was living back in London, she'd listen sleeplessly to the radio turned down low – *Mull of Galloway to Mull of Kintyre, Mull of Kintyre to Ardnamurchan Point* – and picture him out in the squall, a lamp lifted for her arrival.

She'd tracked him down on an old number, badgering away at him with her land-girl spirit as if it was a joke. She was surprised at how readily he gave in. Yes, okay, he'd said, she could come and visit, as long as she travelled as he did on the *Nite-rider*: *Shite-rider* he'd called it, the overnight coach up to Glasgow. And precisely because she wasn't his kind of girl – not beautiful or mysterious enough – she leapt at this chance to prove herself.

At Buchannan station, sick with anticipation, she'd doubted suddenly that he'd be there. But, standing aloof, propped against a concrete pillar, it could only be him, lifting an elbow to acknowledge that he'd seen her. Her legs were gone: if she didn't concentrate she'd topple to one side and he would disappear. She was full of the story: the smell of piss and burning rubber, the boy who'd sat next to her swigging vodka, his shaven head like a croquet ball against her shoulder.

The blue Renault belonged to his mother. The tug of the seat belt, its clasp, his hand on the gear stick, mirror, signal. It was real. And the glorious domesticity of stopping off at Asda, the trolley rattling with two weeks' worth of *Irn Bru*, oats, bog roll, neaps. They were the Bonnie and Clyde of the drudging, pasty-faced shoppers. The booze had an aisle all to itself, and he was expert. This particular malt. Three bottles. Four. A dozen bottles of wine. And the tin cans came in multi-storeys, in stiff plastic wrap, in tartan. This was Scotland! The trolley clanked and bucked on its wheels. At the checkout, though no-one batted an eye, she imagined it must look as if they were having a party.

There was a zero quality to the air on this peninsular that made everything new, her life before, the cave-life of a grub. In three days they'd rustled up a routine: he'd make a pan of porridge in the morning to set them up for a walk that could last all day. He hadn't dissuaded her from tagging along, the knapsack clanking on his back as they climbed up onto the ridge to follow the sheep track, the sea tugging at their periphery, seabirds wheeling from their roosts.

Every half hour or so he'd call a halt, a suitable spot, he'd say, for a *tinnie* break. His rules. They'd hunker down out of the wind, and he'd crack open a can, use her as a shield to roll a fag, its dog-end soggy from his lips, pressed between hers. That first day the sea had been Mediterranean, the blue as vibrant as a mirage or a solder that promised to fuse them together.

Two nights in a row he'd cooked haggis and neaps, and she enthused as if she'd be happy to eat haggis and nothing but. The fire was lit, whisky – though she hadn't acquired a proper taste for it – and Scrabble, at which he excelled.

Ersatz, maieutic, he spelled, arranging his tiles with glee. Once he'd won they got out their books, she, like a cat, alert for the slightest weakening that might allow her to insinuate her way onto his lap.

Two nights running she'd waited for him upstairs, the sleeping bags unzipped on the narrow beds, as if something had been hatched out. Too cold to get properly undressed, she'd bundled herself up, tracing the parallel lines of light through the floorboards where he sat below, waiting, waiting, until the light became a wave that was the morning, bleary at the bare window.

Ardnamurchan Point to Cape Wrath. A resinous mist made it impossible to make out the full extent of the bay. Underfoot the sand was compact and easier going than on the dunes; she was careful to check her distance, as if any moment she might find herself up to her neck in water. She was the only vertical line out here, the wind racing through her like a needle. The slippery patches either side she knew to be bladder-wrack; the *plat, plat* of her feet telling her that the sea couldn't be far off; a flicker of light she took to be the output of a wave. To her left, a sprouting of rock she recognized, the spit of land they'd climbed in daylight. Her hands stopped with relief against the cold surface, and she allowed herself to glance back over her shoulder – no blip on the blurry line of the dunes, no soft footfall. She daren't turn away for more than a moment: the sea was unpredictable, sneaking up, rattling its cans. She secured a foothold and levered herself up onto the sloping surface, up and across, making for the highest spot.

And then she sat. Like Jonah in the Whale, the sea battering at the door. If she sat and waited he would be bound to come. It was human law. She prayed for it. This was how the story would go: he'd capitulate, worry she'd been gone too long – long enough to have learned her lesson – and out he'd come, that slouching walk of his, the lamps of his eyes far sharper than hers.

She could smell him in the arms of the tweed jacket, still damp from this morning's rain, when they'd sheltered in the ruined cottage. He'd been telling her about the clearances – bloody English! – scoffing at how little she knew, clambering over slabs of fallen stone to escape the downpour. She'd followed, crouching next to him in the lee of a wall, exhilarated by proximity, the lucky conspiracy of rain and stone that had brought them here. 'I could live in this place,' she'd said, her face burning as she plotted a life with only the two of them in it: he in his cottage, she in hers.

'You could write,' she'd said, after supper. 'We could come together for meals and walks.'

Something in the air had switched. It was like a flight of starlings, a shoal of fish. He'd chucked back the drink from the bottom of his glass. 'I don't know who you think you are,' he said, grabbing the bottle. 'But you know fuck all.'

She kept very still.

'You talk out of your arse.' He filled his glass again and took a swig, swilled the liquid round. It was late. The windows were black from the night outside and reflected the room so that she could see herself getting to her feet, heading for the porch. 'I'm going for a walk,' she'd said, hoping to jolt him out of it, stuffing her feet into his mother's boots, taking down his jacket.

She drew in her knees, hugged the rubber boots. If only she could strip herself of Englishness, like a shell. The sea slopped and gurgled below as it slithered off and then returned, slithered off then threw its scorn up in her face. She blinked, her eyes stung, blinded for a moment, panicked. Water everywhere, roiling, bitter-tasting, as if there was no option but to give in, drink, be drowned.

Her skin was quick with sweat and cold. She backed off stiffly on her haunches, inch by inch, her breath lodged in her mouth. When she reached down with her leg, it was plunged into a pool that spilled over her boot and made a sock of ice around her foot. The dark was breaking over her head; she was hours from anywhere, from anyone. What a fool to imagine the sea would be on her side! *Sassenach*, it hissed, another word of his she had by heart.

She stumbled out across the strand and met a wall. Her radar was defunct. Where there were dunes before, now there appeared to be mountains, insurmountable. She skirted to the right. There was a fence where there was no fence before, a ditch. She folded herself into it, sinking down. Above, the earth and sky combined into a gyroscope of roaring. So this was where she'd built her house, on sand, on air, on a vacant lot.

Here's the story. She brought it on herself, and no-one will come to gather her up, to take her home, to tell her it is all right. Stupid cow. And only because the story is determined to come right does she get to her feet, snivelling, and stumble her way along the line of the fence. There is a smudge of light, and though she can't be sure she hasn't conjured it, for want of anything else, she intends to follow it. There's an old sailor who lives with his bedridden wife on the hill; a fierce woman in a cottage near the bay, who was at Greenham Common. Never mind the humiliation – she'll throw herself on the mercy of the first stranger to take her in.

All this is jangling in her head when she hits tarmac, and, ahead of her, recognizes the incongruous blank of the carpark noticeboard. She surges forward, tripping over her feet and arrives at the porch door, bursting. The door shudders as she manhandles her way inside. She takes a moment to prise off the boots, unhand herself from the jacket, and stands breathless looking in.

'I got lost,' she gabbles, careful to strip any accusation from her voice.

He hasn't shifted. He raises the glass to sup, lets it drop, swallows. His eyes remain heavy, and they refuse to meet hers.

'It was *Moby Dick* out there,' she says, making a fool of herself. She kneels down, moving on her knees towards the fire, stretching the clumps of her fingers, raw with cold. Something flits across his face. But it is not relief, and it is definitely not love. She edits it out.

The Ballad of Barefoot Bob
by David Swann

The crossroads didn't have a name; everyone just called it The Traffic Lights. Years back, there had been houses and pubs, even a theatre. But it had all collapsed now, and the council had no cash to demolish the slums, so everything lay there rotting.

Bobby liked The Traffic Lights. You could see into houses, through gaps in broken walls. He spent hours studying beds and wallpaper. The paper had gone shiny and was peeling off in wet strips that reminded him of kelp.

Bobby was mad for a bit of kelp. That's what his dad had said when they all went to the Isle of Man together, before the big hoo-hah with the divorce. He remembered throwing weed at his dad in a rock-pool, and his dad splashing around, covered in slime, shouting, 'Beware, Earthlings! We are The Kelpmen!'

Bobby was waiting for his dad's house-mate to emerge from the slum, so he could tell him about the kelp. This house-mate called himself The Thing, and he'd sometimes sit next to Bobby on a wet plank and play the guitar. That was good, when The Thing played guitar. Bobby would gaze into a fire-pit full of mushy cinders while The Thing tuned up, and he'd occasionally sniff the bottles that littered the ground, some still sloshy with dregs.

Bobby sat there now on the wet plank, wondering if any of the scattered bottles had been touched by his dad. He was a lad for the drink, Bobby's dad. He drank 'to make other folk more interesting.' That's what he'd said.

It was rare for Bobby to sit still, as he was doing now. The doctors called him hyperactive, which was another word for Shufflebottom, the name given by his gran. But the wasteland slowed him down, and that's why he came.

He stared at the slum, imagining his dad inside. He had a lot on, his dad. He was getting straight after the divorce, and Bobby hadn't to bother him. Bobby wasn't supposed to bother The Thing, either. But his dad's house-mate usually emerged if Bobby waited long enough.

Here he came now, carrying his smashed-up guitar. 'Hallo, trouble,' he said. 'Can't stay away, eh?'

'Watching the homing-pigeons,' said Bobby. He liked it when the birds went over, how they vanished when they turned. It was only a fleeting moment, and then they were back again. But, in that second when they turned, it seemed like the pigeons weren't anywhere, as if they'd merged with the sky, become a part of its nothing.

The Thing nodded, admiring the circling birds. 'Aye,' he said, 'they know something we've forgotten, those characters.'

Bobby nodded. 'Shall we sing a right good number?'

The Thing settled himself, breathing out booze-fumes. It had been a heavy night, he told Bobby – but how about this, a number he'd made up, specially? A song called 'Bob Loves the Birds, & the Birds Love Bob'? It turned out to be a belter, about a bloke who was brilliant at pigeon-fancying. But wait! It could be a bloke who was brilliant at fancying women. So The Thing's song was clever, it had two meanings. Even better, the bloke was called Bobby, like Bobby.

The Thing played as if he'd been bashed on the fingers with a hammer. But you sang for the singing, not for the tune. That's what he told Bobby.

After singing, they lay on their backs, knackered, watching the pigeons.

'I once threw some kelp at my dad,' said Bobby.

'Oh, aye. What for?'

'Because he'd invaded The Isle of Man.'

The Thing let out a wheezy laugh.

'He'll tell you, if he comes out …'

The Thing shook his head. 'He's sleeping off a big one,' he said. 'But, you never know, The Monarch occasionally visits his dominions.'

'I'll come back later then,' said Bobby.

'Aye,' said The Thing. 'Come back later, and we'll sing another number, lad.'

Bobby got up and re-set the coordinates in his wrist. Then he took off, floating down the street, at a quiet hum.

*

Soon afterwards Bobby re-calibrated the floating mechanism and sped up. He wanted to tell his friend Philip about the song.

He found Philip moping around in a back-alley, wearing a stupid hat.

'Guess what,' he said, 'I'm famous.'

Philip shrugged, like so what?

'In a right good number written by The Thing,' said Bobby.

'As if I know who The Thing is,' said Philip.

'He's my dad's slum-mate. He comes from Chesterfield, and he's a borderline alcoholic because he used to drink in New Mills, on the border between Derbyshire and Cheshire.'

'So?'

'I'm just saying. He isn't a person anymore, only a thing. That's what he told me. He plays this brilliant song called "House of the Flies and Scum."'

'He's probably a mental-case,' said Philip.

Bobby nodded, and decided to copy one of The Thing's

sayings. '*It's all gone to shit, right enough.*' He studied Philip's new hat. It looked like he'd pulled a mitten over his head. 'Do you want to come to my dad's slum? We're not allowed in, but we can sit outside and look.'

'If there's nowt else to do on a wet Wednesday,' Philip grunted.

'Right, next Wednesday. I'll show you some bottles to sniff. And happen The Thing will rub our heads. He does that sometimes. He rubs my head.'

Philip stiffened. 'Nobody can touch my head. Not now.'

Bobby stepped towards him, but Philip flinched.

'Is this to do with that daft hat?' Bobby asked.

Philip gripped the hat. 'Like it's any of your business,' he said, 'but this is secret, Bobby. So cross your heart and hope to die.'

Bobby crossed his heart.

'Promise?'

'Promise.'

Philip took a breath. 'I've got a ringworm on my head.'

'On your actual head?' said Bobby.

Philip nodded.

'Why?'

'There isn't any reason – it's a parasite. Our bodies are full of them.'

'Mine isn't,' said Bobby.

'It is. Invisible ones. But this is visible, so I need a hat.'

'Can I look?'

When Philip shook his head, Bobby wished the hat would fall off. It didn't budge, though. It sat there, as stiff as an oven-glove. Bobby watched carefully to see if the hat was slowly pulsing or giving off a weird light.

'Can it glow in the dark?' Bobby asked him.

Philip sighed, world-weary. His mum had taken to the bottle because Philip's dad kept shagging everybody. And then she'd left them, suddenly. So now Philip was bereft. That was what Bobby's mum called it: bereft. There were loads of words like that now, not only bereft, but derelict and severance.

Bobby shouted words down the street as Philip traipsed away. 'Maintenance!' he cried. 'Decree nisi! Visitation!'

*

Bobby had crossed his heart without hoping to die. This had freed him. He crashed through the door, shouting, 'Mum! Guess what? Philip has a ringworm!'

Bobby's mum glanced up from the sink, where she was squelching a plunger.

'This ringworm, though, Mum! Did you hear?'

'Aye, it were on the radio.'

Bobby reeled backwards, amazed. 'On the *radio*?'

'Course it weren't,' she said, squeezing the blockage. 'Why the hell would they put ringworms on the radio?'

Bobby thought hard. 'I have no answer to that question,' he said.

'Then go and ask your gran, Bobby. Happen she'll know.'

It was her trick to get him out from under the feet, Bobby knew. It was OK, though – his gran would replenish him with precious nutrients.

As he was turning, his mum let out a yelp. 'Your feet, lad! What the hell have you trodden in now?'

He glanced down at his scumbered shoes, then scanned the trail they'd left through their tiny house.

'Christ, Bobby. *Both* feet?'

Bobby gasped. 'They're filthy, them dogs!'

'Honestly. You're ten now. Why don't you watch where you're going?'

'Because my eyes aren't connected to my brain.'

His mum sighed.

'That's what Dad told me. He said my eyes aren't …'

'Listen. Your dad's a drunk. He's out of the picture. Understand?'

But Bobby had noticed some carpet-fluff. 'That fluff looks exactly like the Isle of Man,' he said.

Despite herself, his mother laughed. Then turned serious again. 'And another thing – if he's got a ringworm, don't touch Philip's head. Understand?'

Bobby nodded solemnly.

'Serious as a deacon. Good. Now – find fresh shoes while I clean this mess.'

Bobby went upstairs, serious as a deacon. 'Onward, Christian soldiers!' he chanted as he mounted the steps.

*

Upstairs, Bobby sat in his window, studying the local area. His street was the last in town, and fizzled out into a scrubby park, overshadowed by the moors. This was the park where Mad Dog Malcolm snogged birds and read sci-fi books.

Really, though. Mad Dog Malcolm, he was virtually a god. He had a proper dad, and smoked, and everything.

It was OK if you found Malcolm alone in the park, on your way to gran's. Then he'd talk in the sci-fi voice about robots and over-population. 'Commander Malcolm,' Bobby would say, 'I am a carbon-based landform, and curious about the future.'

'Soon,' Malcolm once said, 'people will be too numerous to live in houses.'

'And where will the earthlings then reside?'

'In old cars, in multi-storeys. And posh folk, they'll get vans.'

'What colour?' Bobby asked.

Malcolm shook his head, sad. 'There won't be *paint*, Bobby. The paint will have run out yonks ago.'

This thought had played on Bobby's mind. No paint. So yesterday at school he'd asked Malcolm about this. But Malcolm had been with his brilliant friends, and he'd pushed Bobby into a hedge. Then the friends watched while Malcolm tonked him about for a bit. Still, that was understandable. Bobby knew he was a handful – his dad always said so.

He re-set the co-ordinates in his wrist. It was time for the perilous mission to his gran's that might well end in disaster.

*

When Malcolm saw Bobby coming, he puffed harder on his fag. 'Sorry about that fuss and bother yesterday,' he said. 'You caught me at a bad time.'

Bobby nodded.

'I warned you, though,' Malcolm frowned. 'Didn't I say about talking in the sci-fi voice at school?'

Bobby was watching a spider scuttle along a crack.

'See,' Malcolm said. 'That's your problem, Bobby – you *gawp*. And why the hell are you only wearing socks?'

Bobby had lost the thread, and was watching a weary pensioner trudge past the park, carrying a brown shopping bag with a broken zip. Bobby re-programmed his eyes to X-Ray Vision, and decided the bag contained bananas and milk. Unless …

'Hey, Malcolm,' said Bobby, 'what if the milk and bananas are only a *front*?'

Malcolm grunted, and walked away, probably to get off with loads of people in somewhere amazing like Manchester.

At his gran's, Bobby stood in the street, hoping to make contact by The Power of Thought Alone. Then the neighbour's daughter asked him if he was constipated, so he decided to knock.

'Shufflebottom,' said his gran, surprised. 'What brings you here, cock?'

'I have come in search of rice pudding,' he replied.

His gran let him in. 'Where the hell are your shoes?' she said.

'My shoes are inoperative,' Bobby explained.

She shook her head for about thirty minutes, then fed him the pudding. 'I reckon you've got hollow legs,' she said.

'Negative. I am a carbon-based landform, not an android.'

'Anne Droyde?' said his gran. 'Who's Anne Droyde?'

Bobby would have explained, but he was still hungry, so he floated off to eat more pudding, this time from the pan, with a ladle. The pudding tasted better with a ladle.

Then it occurred to Bobby: could you fit a whole ladle into your mouth? He marched outdoors, keen to discover.

That was how he came to be found in the street with a ladle in his mouth.

'If it goes in, it comes out,' he told his gran's neighbour. 'Simple physics.'

But she couldn't understand, because he had a ladle in his mouth.

*

Bobby had heard solicitors tell his mum to supply all relevant information. So, at hospital, after the doctor had removed the ladle, he did just that. But as he reached the part about global over-population, the doctor interrupted. 'Next time,' she said, 'use a bigger ladle. One we can't get out.' She patted his head and packed him off. 'But where are your shoes, lad?' she called. 'Why are you wearing socks?'

Bobby stared across the casualty department. 'That,' he said, 'is classified information,' and strode away, whistling. It felt good to have a mouth again – and he'd decided to shout through it.

*

In the precinct, Bobby began shouting through a broadsheet newspaper that he'd rolled up like a trumpet: 'Late final, read all about it! Philip Rawlins has a ringworm!'

That was when Philip came past, wearing his daft new hat.

'Extra! He hasn't got a mum to check his head for parasites, late final!'

Philip stomped off, casting back furious glances. Bobby drew in breath. Just as he was about to start shouting again, he heard: 'Extra! Bobby Grayling's nickname is Hyperactive Spastic. Extra!'

Bobby marched to the flower-beds, where Philip was standing in his daft new hat, brandishing a rolled-up newspaper. When Bobby lunged for Philip, a pensioner pulled the boys apart. 'Thee! In thi socks! And thee' – he said, turning to Philip – 'shouting like a devil! What would thi fathers say?'

'Bobby's dad's an alcoholic who lives in a slum,' said Philip.

Bobby studied the pensioner. It was the bloke with the busted bag, allegedly containing bananas and milk.

'So where's *thy* dad?' the pensioner asked Philip.

'At home.'

The pensioner looked like he'd played Rugby League in the olden days. His ears were bent. He took Philip by the sleeve and bundled Bobby under his arm.

Then the pensioner set off for Philip's house.

*

As they walked, a stink rose through the air.

Philip groaned. 'He's trodden in dog-mess again.'

The pensioner let Bobby slither from his grasp as if he were a wet rugby ball. 'What the hell …?'

Bobby took his sock off.

'The other one, too,' sighed Philip.

'On *both*?' asked the pensioner.

'It's like buses,' Bobby explained. 'When you wait for the bus, and two come at once. Except these are turds.' He took off the other sock and stood there, bare-footed.

'Nay,' said the pensioner, frowning. 'The cold's benna get in, lad.'

'Cold doesn't get in, heat gets out. Simple physics. Eh, Philip?'

The pensioner shook his head. 'Hell-fire,' he said to Philip, 'I bet this lad's teeth are glad when he falls asleep, eh?'

Philip shrugged. 'He can't help it. He's hyperactive.'

'I eat tons of sugar,' said Bobby.

'Out of the packet,' said Philip. 'In fistfuls.'

The pensioner narrowed his eyes. 'So what's your excuse?' he asked Philip.

Philip shrugged.

*

Philip's dad was tousled-looking when he finally answered the door, as if he'd been in a fight. His vest wasn't on straight. His hair had been knocked sideways. 'You've not lost the bloody key *again*?' he growled.

'There's been some bother down the precinct …' the pensioner began.

Philip's dad tried to fasten his belt, which was hanging down like a snake. 'Why's this idiot got bare feet?' he asked.

Bobby felt sorry for Philip's dad, standing there, clueless. 'It's a difficult time, I appreciate that,' he said. 'What with Philip's ringworm, and …'

'*Will you stop mentioning my ringworm?*' snapped Philip. 'I don't keep going on about you being mental, do I?'

Philip's dad twisted his son's arm. '*Look*,' he said. 'I'm busy. Shake hands.'

When they shook hands, Bobby felt how warm and moist Philip's hand was.

'If I've to come down again, there'll be bother,' said Philip's dad, still tying his belt.

'Okay,' said Bobby. 'Come down from where, though?'

Philip's dad made as if to point at upstairs, then reconsidered.

'Hmmm,' said Bobby. 'The curtains are shut.'

'On your *way*,' said Philip's dad.

'Yet it's the afternoon …' Bobby continued.

'And you too,' he warned his son.

'But …' said the pensioner.

Philip's dad turned with a huff and slammed the door.

The pensioner scratched his head.

'We know about your bag,' Bobby told him. 'You're not kidding anyone.'

Philip rearranged his hat, grumpily. 'Don't take him on,' he told the pensioner. 'If you take him on, he'll never leave you alone. Sometimes he knocks on our door at midnight.'

'When thoughts enter my head,' said Bobby.

The pensioner hissed through his false-teeth, and trudged away with his busted bag. Bobby shook his head, saddened. 'Milk and bananas,' he muttered. 'As if, eh?'

Philip didn't respond. He was watching the upstairs window. Bobby followed his gaze. The glass was mucky. The curtains weren't straight. An ornament had fallen over.

'I surmise,' said Bobby, 'that your father is engaged in a sordid act with a floozy.'

'It's got nothing to do with you.'

'They'll be at it like rabbits, I expect,' said Bobby.

That was when Philip jumped on Bobby and began pounding him with his moist, sickly fists. The boys rolled around, fighting, whispering savagely into each other's ears.

'At least I'm not mental.'

'Yeah, but you're half-worm.'

'At least my dad's not a derelict.'

'Yeah, but your mum is.'

Slowly, they began to fight less effectively, as if under water. When they whispered, their voices sounded worn-out. In the end, they were reduced to lying on their backs, staring up at the sky, sobbing gently.

Eventually Philip wiped his eyes. His hat had been knocked off. Beneath it, he had an old man's hair, grey and patchy. The ringworm didn't look like a worm. It looked soft and white, bleached like the grass around a moorland bog.

'Sorry,' he said.

'That's okay,' said Bobby. 'Fighting makes an appetite.'

Philip covered the ringworm with his hat. He stared up at the window, his eyes burning. 'Your problem, Bobby,' he said, 'is you get everything mixed up. You ought to be bothered about *your* dad, not mine. You ought to make your dad come out and talk to you.'

'He will, when he's less busy.'

'Less busy? He lives in a slum.'

'There's no need to be rude,' said Bobby. 'It isn't my fault your dad shags everybody except your mum, Philip.'

'You,' said Philip, 'you take the rotten biscuit, you.'

Bobby nodded. 'And the wrapper and the box. That's what my dad said.'

Philip tightened his hat. 'Someone that crackers, he'd know all about biscuits.'

Bobby laughed. Then he stopped laughing and studied the sky. 'I'm going to sing another number with The Thing. Do you want to come?'

'I'd rather eat my own young,' said Philip.

*

The fight must have broken his mechanisms. Unable to float, Bobby had to walk back to The Traffic Lights. When he finally got there, he was knackered, and the Monarch was still absent from his dominions, so he sat on the plank until The Thing came out, loaded with beer-cans and his beat-up guitar. Then they sang the birds song again.

Afterwards, Bobby told The Thing it was a good song, but…

'But you'd rather see your dad, eh?'

Bobby shuffled on the plank.

'Maths, eh?' said The Thing, putting down his beer-can. 'Multiply every song ever written, it'd never add up to one dad.' He struggled to his feet and rubbed Bobby's head. 'Listen: if he refuses to come out, it's him, not you. Got me?'

Bobby nodded. He watched The Thing trudge back to the slum. Then it went quiet, until the shouting started. It was his dad's voice he could hear, slurred and angry. When his dad's voice got loud, he covered his ears, but it didn't work, so he took a pull on The Thing's can.

The beer tasted worse than Bobby had expected, but interesting, so he finished the first can and then forced down another, until his head was fizzing. Were other folk becoming more interesting yet? It was hard to tell, since there was no-one else there, only smashed-up houses. Without their roofs, the houses looked as if they'd been laid bare, like Philip's head. There was nothing covering their secrets anymore.

It was because his brain didn't connect to his mouth. That's why he said mad things, and made his friends cry. That's why Mad Dog Malcolm dragged him through bushes.

He shut his eyes to stop everything spinning – and when he opened them again, The Thing was standing above him, unsteadily.

'Is my dad still busy?'

'Exceptionally,' said The Thing.

'But maybe he'll be finished soon?'

'Maybe,' said The Thing. He sat on the plank beside Bobby and took up the guitar. Above, the pigeons circled, making Bobby even dizzier. It wasn't just their motion, but their mystery. Sometimes the birds found their way home all the way from Belgium. The Thing was right: they knew things people had forgotten.

In what felt like the far distance, The Thing was singing a number called 'The Ballad of Barefoot Bob,' all about this really hard lad who walked over glaciers and through streams of burning lava, and his feet never felt it.

Bobby fell off the plank, and lay on his back, staring at the sky, listening to The Thing's song. He let his mind go up to the homing-pigeons, until it was high above, flying out over the wasteland.

Below was the crossroads, with its missing roofs and walls, its stained mattresses and broken bottles. But the pigeons just whizzed over as if none of it had anything to do with them.

Then they turned their wings away from the light, and Bobby followed them, into that fleeting second when they vanished.

Contributors' Notes

Judith Allnatt is an acclaimed novelist and short story writer. Her four novels *A Mile of River*, *The Poet's Wife*, *The Moon Field* and *The Silk Factory* have been variously featured as a Radio 5 Live Book of the Month and short-listed for the Portico prize for Literature and for the East Midlands Book Award. Short stories have featured in the Bridport Prize Anthology, on Radio 4 and in the Commonwealth Short Story Collection.

Jenn Ashworth is a novelist and short-story writer based in Lancaster, Lancashire. Her latest novel, *Fell*, is published by Sceptre. She is currently working on a memoir-in-essays that explores illness and creativity.

Des Barry has written three novels for Jonathan Cape: *The Chivalry of Crime*, *A Bloody Good Friday* and *Cressida's Bed*. His alter-ego David Enrique Spellman produced *Far South* for Serpent's Tail. His shorter prose has been published in *The New Yorker*, *Granta,* at www.3ammagazine.com and in anthologies *Wales, Half Welsh, Sea Stories* and *London Noir*. He tweets from @farsouthproject.

Laurie Cusack is currently writing a collection of short stories about the Irish for his Creating Writing Ph.D at Leicester University. He has had several short stories published. Laurie pickled his mind and his liver many moons ago: 'One for the wobbly?' used to be his drinking cry.

Louis de Bernières was born in 1954 and was seduced into becoming a wine lover by Omar Khayyam, his father, a French family near Saumur, and a large number of

Greeks. He intends to be buried with a pipe into his coffin so that a bottle of Burgundy can be poured down it on significant anniversaries.

Jane Feaver is a novelist and short story writer. She was shortlisted for the Author's Club Best First Novel Award and the Dimplex Prize for *According to Ruth* (2007), and for the Edge Hill Short Story Prize for *Love Me Tender* (2009). She is a lecturer in Creative Writing at the University of Exeter.

Cathy Galvin is a journalist, editor and writer with roots in London, Cornwall and Connemara. Her work has appeared in national and international journals. Her poetry pamphlets, *Black and Blue* and *Rough Translation*, are published by The Melos Press. She is founder and director of the short story organisation The Word Factory. Website: www.cathygalvin.com

Alison Moore's short fiction has been included in *Best British Short Stories* and *Best British Horror* anthologies and broadcast on BBC Radio. Her first novel, *The Lighthouse*, was shortlisted for the Man Booker Prize and the National Book Awards, winning the McKitterick Prize. Her fourth novel, *Missing*, is out now, and her first book for children, *Sunny and the Ghosts*, will be published in November 2018.

Kate North lives in Cardiff and teaches at Cardiff Metropolitan University. She writes fiction and poetry. Her latest collection is *The Way Out* (Parthian, 2018). Her website is www.katenorth.co.uk.

Bethan Roberts has published four novels: *The Pools*, *The Good Plain Cook*, *My Policeman*, and *Mother Island*, which was the recipient of a Jerwood Fiction Uncovered prize. Her short fiction has been awarded the Society of Authors' Olive Cook Prize and the Royal Academy Pin Drop Award. Chatto & Windus will publish her new novel, *Graceland*, which tells the story of Elvis Presley and his mother, in 2019.

Jane Roberts's short fiction is published in a variety of anthologies and journals, has been shortlisted for Bridport and Fish Prizes, and won Bloomsbury Writers' and Artists' Flash Fiction 2013. After many years of wine-buying experience at auctions, she began her Wine and Spirits Education Trust (WSET) journey in 2012, leading on to freelance wine commentary and editorial work. Twitter: @JaneEHRoberts. Website: janeehroberts.wordpress.com

Hannah Stevens writes short stories and flash fiction. Her pamphlet, *Without Makeup and Other Stories,* was published in 2012 and she has published stories in various print anthologies and literary journals. She has a Ph.D in Creative Writing and teaches Creative Writing workshops in a range of educational settings and the community. She currently lives in Leicester with her house-rabbit Agatha.

Karen Stevens is a Senior Lecturer in English and Creative Writing at the University of Chichester, in West Sussex. She has a special interest in the novel and short fiction. Her short stories have been published in *The Big Issue, Pulp Net, Panurge New Fiction, Mouth Ogres, Dreaming Beasts, Fish Publishing, Riptide, Salt Publishing*. Her edited collection of essays, *Writing a First Novel*, was published by Palgrave Macmillan in 2014.

Michael Stewart's debut novel, *King Crow*, was published in January 2011 by Bluemoose Books. It is the winner of the *Guardian*'s Not the Booker Award and has been selected as a recommended read for World Book Night. He is also the author of *Couples*, a book of poetry, described by Ian McMillan as 'inspired' and 'ingenious,' *Café Assassin* (a novel), and a short story collection, *Mr Jolly*. His new novel, *Ill Will*, is published by HarperCollins. Find out more about him here: www.michael-stewart.org.uk or find him on Twitter @headspam.

David Swann likes all beverages, except Bovril. He teaches at Chichester University, and was shortlisted for the Ted Hughes Award for his collection *The Privilege of Rain* (Waterloo Press, 2010), about his residency in a prison.

Jonathan Taylor's books include the novel *Melissa* (Salt, 2015), the memoir *Take Me Home* (Granta, 2007), and the short story collection *Kontakte and Other Stories* (Roman, 2013). He is editor of the anthology *Overheard: Stories to Read Aloud* (Salt, 2012). Since starting to co-edit this anthology, his alcohol intake has plummeted.

Melanie Whipman's debut collection, *Llama Sutra* (2016), was long listed for the Edgehill Prize and won the Rubery International Prize for short story collections. Her stories have been published in various literary magazines and broadcast on Radio 4. She is an Associate Lecturer at the University of Chichester, leads creative writing workshops in Farnham, and is commissioning editor for *The Story Player*. She has a PhD in Creative Writing.

Sue Wilsea's work is with words, whether that's writing, performing or teaching. Her fiction has been widely published and broadcast with her first collection of short stories, *Staying Afloat*, being published by Valley Press in 2012 and her second, *Raw Material*, in November 2016. The latter was recently long-listed for the Edge Hill prize. She completed an MA (Distinction) in Creative Writing at Newcastle in 2014.